Be a Genie in
Six Easy Steps

LINDA CHAPMAN and STEVE COLE

Be a Genie in Six Easy Steps

HARPER

An Imprint of HarperCollins*Publishers*

Be a Genie in Six Easy Steps

www.harpercollinschildrens.com

Library of Congress Cataloging-in-Publication Data
Chapman, Linda.
Be a genie in six easy steps / by Linda Chapman & Steve Cole. —
1st ed.
    p. cm.
Summary: Four new stepsiblings move from London to an out-of-
the-way English village, where they discover a book—inhabited by
a grouchy bookworm—that promises to make the reader a wish-
granting genie.
ISBN 978-0-06-125219-8
[1. Genies—Fiction. 2. Magic—Fiction. 3. Stepchildren—Fiction.
4. England—Fiction.] I. Cole, Steve. II. Title.
PZ7.C3717Be 2009   2009014271
[Fic]—dc22   CIP
                                                          AC

Typography by Andrea Vandergrift
09 10 11 12 13   LP/RRDB   10 9 8 7 6 5 4 3 2 1
❖
First Edition

*This book is dedicated to
the memory of the author E. Nesbit.
Her wonderful books about magic
and ordinary family life inspired us both
to write this story in tribute—a kind of
"Four" Children and It for today's readers.*

Prologue

In a dim and distant place, long ago . . .

The forgotten room stood in the farthest, shadowy reaches of the ancient library. Nobody went there. There was a large lock on the huge oak door to stop anyone who might try, but nobody ever had.

The students, the scholars, even those who staffed the marble halls of learning, simply accepted the room's existence and ignored it. It was almost as if the room itself did not want to be disturbed. As if it could cast a spell on anyone who came near, moving them gently along: Nothing to see in here, nothing to see . . .

In any case, never once did a single soul imagine what might lurk inside the forgotten room. The answer was simple and, on the surface, not at all surprising.

Books.

Big books. Small books. Middle-size ones, too. They sat in stacks or weighed down shelves or littered the marble floor, their hard edges softening beneath a blanket of thick dust. Squeezed in among them were parchments and pamphlets and faded, crumbling scrolls.

The room had no windows, and the locked door offered the only way in or out—to human eyes at least. But on the other side of the door, the smooth oak was carved with runes in strange shapes, like the shadows of weird, unknown creatures; a powerful charm, designed to protect the precious books and scraps of knowledge gathered here.

Because those who had built the forgotten room foretold a time when it might be remembered.

And, one cold fourth-century day, that time finally arrived.

It was announced by the eager thump of filthy feet on the marble, and shouts of alarm.

"What's all the noise? Keep back, you can't—!"

The elderly librarian by the door was knocked to the ground as thieves and bandits poured in from the streets and spilled into the spotless chambers. They upturned tables and chests, scattered the ordered contents in all directions, crushing precious scrolls and trampling parchments underfoot, dragging the heavy volumes from the shelves and stuffing them into sacks.

The door to the forgotten room seemed to shrink into shadow, as if trying to hide. But one man knew where to find it. Eyes agleam, he produced a key from around his neck. It fit into the lock perfectly. Silently, followed by just a few others, he slipped through the door.

And in less than ten minutes, the room was as bare as a bone, picked clean.

All except for one book. A tall, very thin book with a dark leather cover. It lay in a corner, abandoned in dust.

Suddenly a trace of gold about the cover seemed to glow in the light and caught the eye of a lingering thief. Why not take that last book, too? It was small; it would weigh little on his back.

He snatched it up and ran. Over the noise of screaming onlookers and the pounding of his heart, the thief could not hear the soft and slightly curious sounds coming from within the pages.

The whispering sound of tiny jaws, chomping through ancient paper. The quiet rustling of someone very small who had no idea of the long, long journey that lay ahead of him . . .

Chapter One

"Your mum's going to go crazy!" cried Milly Worthington, staring at the heavy box of books on the kitchen table.

"I know," muttered Jason, her stepbrother, looking up from his Sudoku puzzle. A few tattered paperbacks spilled out of the box onto the pine tabletop. "She told your dad not to buy any more books."

"Watch out!" Mr. Worthington cried, breezing back into the kitchen. "More books coming through!"

Jason and Milly ducked as another cardboard box sailed over their heads to land with a crash on top of the first.

"Dad!" Milly exclaimed.

"There're still four more boxes to bring in," Mr. Worthington said, ignoring his daughter's protest. He swung around and almost collided with Michael, Milly's older brother, who was slouching in the kitchen with his Game Boy. "Going to give me a hand, Michael?"

"Nope!" Michael threw himself into a chair, his dark

shaggy fringe falling into his eyes, his thumbs jabbing rapidly at the keys.

"I'll help," Jason volunteered.

"Me too!" Milly said, jumping to her feet.

"Oh, no, you won't!"

Jason looked up to find his mum, Ann, had come into the kitchen. "Those books can *stay* out there," she said firmly.

Mr. Worthington's face fell. "Oh, come on, Ann, at least have a look at them. There was a clearance sale at that big old house on the hill; it must have had a really impressive library. . . ."

"We need to talk." Ann Worthington marched him through to the dining room. The door shut with a bang but it didn't stop their voices from carrying through the walls.

"For goodness sake, Mark, we've already got a whole shop full of books that need sorting and pricing, and we open for business in a week!"

"I know, but I'll bet I got some real bargains—"

"We make decisions *together*!" Jason could hear the hurt in his mum's voice. "Moving out of London to open a bookshop wasn't just your dream—it was mine as well. . . ."

"Blah, blah, blah," Michael muttered, turning up the volume on his Game Boy.

Milly sidled up to Jason. "Shall we take a stroll, young man?" she said, putting on a quavery voice like an old woman. Milly loved drama and often spoke in funny voices. At her old school she had very nearly been the youngest lead ever in the end-of-year play at just eight years old. But then they had all moved here to Moreways Meet. . . .

"Yeah, let's get out of here," Jason agreed.

They slipped out through the back door.

The April air outside was cool on their faces. Behind the house, the misty Malvern hills rose in the distance. Two song thrushes were warbling in a nearby tree.

Milly's eyes darted around. "What should we do?" she said in her normal voice. Her gaze fell on the open trunk of her dad's car. Four cardboard boxes were piled up beside it. "I know! Why don't we have a look at the rest of those books Dad bought, see if there *is* anything good."

Jason sighed. "What's the point?"

"You heard what Dad said; there could be all sorts of books in those boxes!" Milly dragged him enthusiastically over to the car. "Come on, quick, before your mum burns them all."

"Paper bursts into flame at two hundred and thirty-two degrees Celsius," Jason noted.

Milly shot him a look. "I'll bet there're loads of boring facty books here that even *you'll* like." Crouching down, her dark ponytail falling over one shoulder, she flung the first box open and started to sort through the titles. "*My Life in Politics, How to Rear a Beagle* . . . nope, nope, nope." Milly threw the books carelessly out of the box. "Nothing good so far."

Jason sat back on his heels. He could still hear the sound of angry voices through the dining room window. "I thought moving in together was supposed to make everyone happy," he sighed. "But it's been four weeks now, and everyone's sad. My mum and your dad argue the whole time, and Michael and Jess are missing London so much that they're in the world's longest bad moods."

Milly nodded. "I wish we *were* still in London because then I could have been—"

"Dorothy in *The Wizard of Oz*," Jason broke in. "I know." He'd heard his stepsister moan about not being Dorothy practically a thousand times.

"It's just *so* not fair!" Milly declared, tossing her hair back as she pulled the rest of the books out of the box. "I'd have gotten to sing and dance *and* act. It would have been brill—" She broke off as she reached the bottom of the box. "Hey, there's a really funny little book down here, Jase. Look!"

Jason peered into the box. A thin book with a dark leather cover was lying on the bottom. It looked old. Older than any book he had ever seen.

A title was etched into the cover in ornate gold writing. Jason frowned. It was hard to make out the exact words because the letters had so many swirls and curls at the ends. "*The Genie Handbook*," he read out. "*Grant Wishes Like an Expert in Six Easy Steps.*"

"What?" Milly was taken aback. "It tells you how to be a genie?"

"As if!" Jason laughed. "It must just be a storybook." He took it out. For such a slim book, it was strangely heavy. He put it down on the ground between them.

Milly opened it. "Oh," she sighed. "It's written in a foreign language."

Jason saw she was right. He wasn't sure that the words were even printed; they looked almost handwritten, with funny squiggles all over the place.

"Shame," said Milly. "It sounded like a really good book." She jumped to her feet and put her hands together. "Your wish is my command!" she said, giving a dramatic bow. "I'd be a cool genie, wouldn't I, Jase?"

Jason smiled at her, but there was something bothering him. Suddenly he realized what it was. "Wait a sec. Why's the title in English if the rest of the book is in another language? That doesn't make sense."

Milly looked surprised. "You're right. Maybe there are

some English words farther on."

The paper was soft and old, and as the first few pages flicked through her fingers they made a gentle rustling sound. But as she turned more and more, a new noise began to come from the book.

A chomping, wriggling noise.

It seemed to come from deep within the pages, getting louder and louder.

"What's that sound?" Milly said. "What . . . ?" She broke off as the book started to tremble beneath her fingers. She snatched them away, and the book fell shut. It lay there, quiet and still again.

For a moment she and Jason both just stared at it.

"Did . . . did you see that?" Milly whispered, gazing at the book as if it was about to jump up and bite her.

Jason nodded. "It shook. It definitely shook, all by itself."

"And it made a noise." Milly gulped.

"But books *don't* shake and make noises," said Jason. "Maybe it got so squashed at the bottom of the box, the pages were expanding. . . ."

"Not *everything* has a brainbox explanation." Milly looked at him. Her blue eyes widened. "What if . . . what if this book is magic?"

"Magic?" Jason echoed. "A *magic* book?" Crouching

down beside the book, he took a handful of pages in his right hand and cautiously started to flick through them, letting them fall one at a time. The book started to tremble. "It's happening again!" he gasped.

"Keep going!" Milly exclaimed as the same strange chomping, wriggling noise they'd heard before started up again.

Jason let the pages fall faster and faster. The book began shaking so much it almost jumped out of his grip. Then there was a ripping noise—and a hole appeared in the middle of the book.

And then *something* popped out from inside it! A tiny wriggling something, its brown, segmented body curling from side to side.

"Ugh!" Jason cried. "It's a maggot!"

Milly gasped as, before their eyes, the tiny wriggly creature started to *grow*. "I never saw a maggot do *that* before!"

It grew bigger and bigger, until suddenly it was the size of Jason's thumb.

"*Maggot?*" it squawked. "Maggot indeed!"

"Agh!" Jason sent gravel flying as he jumped backward. "A *talking* maggot!"

Straining with effort, the creature wriggled out a little farther from its hole. It looked almost speechless with fury.

"Do these handsome, regal features look like a maggot's to you?"

Jason couldn't actually find many features to judge. The might-be-a-maggot's mouth was a simple black line, crinkled in disapproval. Its two dark eyes flicked crossly from Jason to Milly under the specks of its brows. "Well?"

"Actually, you look more like a worm," Milly admitted. She gasped as she made the connection. "Are you a *bookworm*?"

"A bookworm!" The creature drew himself up haughtily. "I am a good deal more than just a bookworm, young lady. Still, if you can see me that must mean you believe in magic at least. Now, come on, what do you mean by disturbing me like this? Explain yourselves!" His beady eyes swiveled impatiently from one to the other. "Hurry up! I'm waiting!"

Chapter Two

Michael was finally about to beat the end-of-level monster when his Game Boy was yanked from his hands. "Hey!" he yelled, looking up to find both Milly and Jason in his face. "Gimme it back!"

"No!" Milly switched off his game and plonked it on the kitchen table.

"Are you *mental*?" Michael cried. "It took me *two hours* to get that far. . . ."

"Michael!" Milly exclaimed. "This is important. We . . ."

The kitchen door opened. Milly spun around, but it was just Jess, her fourteen-year-old stepsister. She came into the room, shoulder-length honey-blond hair perfectly straightened, not a strand out of place.

"What's up?" She frowned as she noticed Jason's and Milly's pale faces. "You two look like you've seen a ghost."

"Not a ghost," said Milly, her eyes wide. "A worm!"

"A really angry one!" said Jason, holding up the old book. "It's in here!"

Michael stared at him in disbelief. "You two stopped me from getting my highest-ever score to show me a squashed *worm*?" He paused. "Actually, that does sound quite cool. Get it out, then."

"It's not squashed!" cried Milly. "It's alive and wriggly and cross 'cause we've woken it up and—"

Jess shook her head. "Oh, not *another* of your dumb made-up plays, Milly."

"Show them, Jason!" said Milly. "Let them see for themselves!"

Jason gulped. "Is it safe? He seemed really angry. . . ."

"Guys," said Michael, scowling, "you have until the count of five to come up with something impressive enough to stop me from killing you. One . . ."

Jason hurriedly opened up the book.

"Two . . ."

Jason and Milly started turning the pages, but gingerly, as if worried the book might bite them.

"Three . . ."

Milly started turning the pages faster. "There!" she squealed. "Look, there!"

Michael blinked and leaned forward, as did Jess.

"What?" Michael said.

"Don't you see him?" asked Milly.

Michael frowned. There was *something* there—a sort of pinky-brown shadow in the middle of one of the pages. Probably a prehistoric jam stain or a wiped booger or something, he decided. "Four," he went on.

"Be quiet a second!" Jess stared at the open book. "I heard something! Like a little squeaking voice."

Michael blinked as the shadow seemed to shift on the page. With a shock, he realized *he* could hear a little voice too:

". . . dear, oh, dear, we're never going to get anywhere at this rate; what's wrong with the pair of them? Don't tell me they're so dim they don't believe in magic . . . ?"

Michael's mouth went dry. "Jason," he said slowly, "how are you making that voice?"

"I'm *not* making it!" Jason insisted.

"You are!" said Michael. "You've got to be."

"How could I be while I'm talking to you?" Jason stabbed a finger at the page. "It's *that* thing talking!"

Jess stared at the book. "It—it's getting louder!"

"Hard-boiled heads, that's what they've got! It happens to certain SILLY people as they get older. . . . Well, I'm not waiting around all day, you know! I'm not going to BEG anyone to believe in me! Certainly not! *I* beg? I, who have consorted with princes and popes and—"

"What the . . . ?" Michael stared at the shadow in the

book as it grew more solid and began to curl like a wriggly question mark. He took a step back, shaking his head. "No way. This can't be happening!"

"But it is," Jess breathed, crouching down. "It's a talking worm! Look, its little eyes are blinking!"

"LITTLE EYES? Of all the cheek!" The voice was getting louder and louder and crosser and crosser as the shape grew. "I've seen more things with these eyes than you could possibly imagine in a million years. . . ."

Michael clapped his hands over his ears. "Nooooo!" he moaned. "This is mega-mental. There can't really be a talking worm in a book. There just *can't* be!"

Milly yanked his hands down. "Michael! Look. You can see him." Her eyes shone. "Oh, I'm so glad! I know you *think* you're too cool to believe in magic—"

Michael stared at the worm. "I believe I've gone grade-A fruit loops!"

The bookworm stared back with beady eyes. "Fruit? Loops? In all my days I've never met ANYONE as dim and as dense, silly, and senseless as you, boy!"

Michael opened and shut his mouth. For the first time in his life he was lost for words.

"What is this book?" said Jess. "Where did you get it?"

"It's called *The Genie Handbook*, and it came from the big old house on the hill," Milly replied. "It says on the cover that it teaches you how to be a genie in six steps."

"But how can it?" Jess said.

"Maybe we should go to the den." Jason looked nervously at the bookworm. "If Mum or Mark comes into the kitchen and finds us with . . . *that* . . . !"

"That?" squawked the worm furiously. "'That' indeed?"

"Shhh!" Jess said, half expecting her mum and Mark to come running. "You're right, Jase. Let's go to the den."

"And let's have a closer look at this book," Michael added. He picked it up gingerly and looked all around it for any signs of wires, projectors, anything dodgy. But there was only the old, crumbling paper and the worn leather cover. Michael gulped. The worm scowled at him as he finished his inspection.

"Here." Michael passed the book to Jason. "You found it; you carry it!"

They hurried along the hallway. There was an old wooden door under the stairs. Michael pulled it open and they piled down the rickety staircase inside. The den was a large, ramshackle space at the bottom, strewn with old clothes and games, older furniture and half unpacked boxes. There was a saggy sofa, an old chair, several beanbags, and an ancient stereo. Jason put the book down on a packing case.

"Who *are* you?" Jess asked the worm.

"My name," replied the bookworm loftily, "is Skribbaleum El Lazeez Ekir."

Michael frowned. "Skribble-what?"

"Skribble!" Milly grinned. "That's a cool name for a bookworm."

"I have already told you I am *not* a bookworm," said Skribble sharply. "I am, in fact, a . . ."

He suddenly stopped.

"Well?" asked Milly eagerly.

Skribble cleared his throat, and his tone changed. "I *am*, in fact, a bookworm." He nodded vigorously. "Yes, yes, full marks to you all, you clever children. You've spotted it. I am a bookworm. Yes, that's exactly what I am."

"Except that you're not," Jason pointed out logically. "Because a *real* bookworm is a beetle larva, and they can't talk, and—"

"Begone with your beetles, boy!" Skribble exclaimed. "Of course I am no *ordinary* bookworm. . . ." He paused impressively. "I am a *magical* one."

"Glad we've cleared that up." Michael felt like he was in a dream. "So, you're expecting us to believe you're a talking magical bookworm who's been stuck in that book for, what . . . ?"

"About two thousand years," said Skribble. "Give or take a century or two."

Milly gaped. "You've been shut away all that time?"

"Well, I may have peeped out now and again, but I can only be seen by those who believe magic is possible," Skribble replied. "This handbook was once part of the Great Genie Library of Magical Muses, but two thousand years ago the library was ransacked by thieves. This book, along with many other magical works, was hidden in the Human Realm until the thieves thought it safe to collect." He sighed. "But they never did. Here in your world it has been bought and sold, stolen and recovered umpteen times over the centuries." He tutted and looked around. "Now I appear to have ended up here. . . ."

Michael narrowed his eyes. "Are you *sure* you're not a special effect?"

Skribble frowned. "I am extremely special and effective, if that is what you mean!"

"But you *must* be computer generated or something. . . ." Michael turned to the others. "This *so* can't be happening!"

"I *am* here in front of your eyes and I *am* real," Skribble said in a tone that would accept no arguments. "So . . ." He looked around at them all. "Are you going to introduce yourselves?"

Milly pushed Michael to one side and crouched beside Skribble. "I'm Milly and this nut is my brother, Michael."

"I'm Jason," Jason put in. "And this is my sister, Jess."

Jess gave the bookworm a dazed smile. "Michael and Milly are our stepbrother and stepsister," Jason explained.

"My dad has just gotten married to Jess and Jason's mum," Milly added.

"Your tribal arrangements are of no matter to me," Skribble said impatiently. He peered around at them all. "How old are you?"

"I'm eight," Milly replied. "Jason is nine, Michael's thirteen, and Jess is fourteen."

"And you want to become genies?" Skribble said slowly.

"Yeah!" Milly and Jason exclaimed.

Michael snorted. "Genies! Why would we want to be genies?"

Milly smiled sweetly at him. "Okay then, Michael. You just go back to your dumb video games while the rest of us do magic and have all our wishes come true and live an amazingly brilliant life without you—loser!"

Michael hesitated. "What about you, Jess?" he appealed to his stepsister. "You don't really believe in this kids' stuff, do you?"

Jess looked embarrassed. "There's no harm in going along with it, is there?" She cleared her throat. "For Jason's and Milly's sakes, I mean."

Michael stared at her.

"Hmm . . . You might just fit my needs," Skribble muttered thoughtfully, studying them. "Yes, you might do very well." His tone changed. "Well, if that's what you want, what are you waiting for? Stop wasting time and start reading the introduction of this magnificent manuscript. I'll be back when you've finished."

With that, he vanished inside his little hole in the old, discolored paper.

"Wow!" gasped Milly. "Isn't he brilliant?"

From inside the book there was a faint rustle, as if a tiny head was nodding in approval.

Suddenly the book began to shake. "What's happening?" Jess asked in alarm.

"It did this before!" Jason exclaimed. "I think it means something magic's going on!"

Chapter Three

The children stared at the book as it juddered and shook. After a few seconds, it jerked upward and fell back, lying open at the first page. Words had formed there in swift, bold strokes of indigo ink, the color of night skies in summer.

Jason leaned forward. "We can read it," he said to Milly. "It's in English now!"

"Read it out loud, then," Milly urged him.

"*YOU WHO ARE WITNESS*
TO THESE WORDS!

"*Welcome to* The Genie Handbook. *If you are able to read this script, then rejoice—for your mind is open and you see things as they truly are. This talent will serve you well as you strive to complete the many tasks ahead.*

"*This book is unlike any other. If you are*

worthy, it will show you wonders. If you are wise, you will learn to do wondrous things. If you are meant to, you will master many magical arts. And most magical of all, you will learn to grant WISHES for those lesser mortals who summon you.

"YOU WHO ARE WITNESS TO THESE WORDS! From this point forth, you fashion your own fate. If you have a hungry heart and a will to win . . . If you are sure enough of your direction in life to follow your dream . . . you shall surely sail serenely through the six steps of apprenticeship and become a GENIE. . . ."

"A *genie!*" Milly gasped. "Then it's really true! This book could make us *all* into genies!"

"I thought people were meant to find lamps with genies inside," Jess said, frowning. "That's how it is in stories. People don't usually become genies themselves!"

"But this isn't a story!" Milly's eyes shone. "Oh, wow! We could all become genies and grant wishes!"

"We'd be able to wish for anything we wanted!" said Jason.

Jess caught her breath. "We could wish ourselves back to London!"

Michael began to look interested. "You mean if this book really worked, we could have our lives back the way they were before we came to Moreways Meet?"

Jess closed her eyes. "My own bedroom instead of having to share, being back with all my mates . . ."

"I could have a signal on my mobile!" said Michael, suddenly excited. "And Gamez-R-Us just around the corner. I could go to all my old after-school clubs. . . ."

Jason nodded. "I could see my friends and teachers."

"And I could go back and be Dorothy!" said Milly. "What are we waiting for?"

Michael caught himself. *What am I thinking? As if we could really become genies.* "We're waiting to wake up," he told Milly. "Nice dream, but I'm telling you—stuff like this just doesn't happen!"

Milly ignored him and quickly turned the page. One big red word caught all their attention straightaway.

WARNING!

The contents of this magical handbook are as precious as a first heartbeat and as powerful as the Earth's spin. Before you begin, you must make a solemn, binding vow never to share its knowledge, to speak of its existence to others, or to use its great teachings unwisely.

"Well, get on with it then!" came a crotchety voice. Skribble burst out through the page. "You've read the introduction; you want to become genies. You must now take your solemn, binding vow." He looked suddenly cagey. "Repeat after me: To be a genie is my heart's desire."

Jason frowned. "But that's not vowing we'll keep everything secret like the book said."

"Who knows best?" Skribble demanded. "Me—a clever and distinguished being who's been living inside this book for almost two thousand years—or you, an idle idiot with a brain full of beetles?"

But my heart's desire isn't to be a genie, thought Jess. *It's to go back to London.*

Then she stopped herself. She was believing in all this way too easily—as if she was just a kid again. Michael had to be right; this was all a clever trick. Wasn't it?

You can't take the chance, whispered a voice at the back of her mind. She looked at the prissy little bookworm, so solid and real in this mysterious book. *Say whatever it wants you to—what have you got to lose? If you were a genie, you could put your life back the way it was. . . .*

Michael nudged her. "Come on. The sooner we say it, the sooner nothing will happen and I can prove this is all just rubbish."

"I imagine you know a very great deal about rubbish, you young ruffian!" Skribble sniffed. "Now, come on, all together: To be a genie is my heart's desire."

"To be a genie is my heart's desire," they all chorused obediently.

A shiver ran through the book and a spark of light jumped across its cover.

"Whoa!" said Michael, looking spooked.

"Splendid," chortled Skribble. "*Now* all you need do is tell the book you solemnly vow never to share its knowledge, to speak of its existence to others, or to use its great teachings unwisely."

Jason frowned. "But that's what we were going to do in the first place!"

Skribble seemed to be smirking. "You'd better get on with it, then, hadn't you!"

They looked at each other, shrugged, and then said: "We solemnly vow never to share your knowledge, to speak of your existence to others, or to use your great teachings unwisely."

Nothing happened. Not a single page of the book moved.

"Hmmm," said Skribble, putting his head to one side and frowning.

"What is it?" asked Jess.

"The book doesn't appear to be convinced," Skribble replied. He poked the book with his tail but still nothing happened. "You are going to have to try harder to make it believe that you mean what you say."

"It's hard to sound like we mean stuff when we have to use silly, old-fashioned words," Milly complained.

"What about if we say the vow in words *we* would use, then?" Jason suggested.

"Would that work?" Jess asked Skribble.

"For goodness sake! Don't you children ever think for yourselves?" the bookworm blustered. "You have brains! Use them!"

Jess looked at him. "You don't know, do you?"

"How dare you!" Skribble cried.

"Don't let's argue," said Milly. "I want to start doing some magic." She turned to her brother. "Can you think of something to say, Michael?"

Jess nodded. "Something that means the same but in our own words?"

Michael looked at her suspiciously. "You really want to believe this magic genie stuff could actually be true, don't you?"

Jess's cheeks reddened, but she met his gaze. "Don't you?" she said quietly. "If you didn't believe just a bit, you wouldn't have seen Skribble at all."

Michael looked away. He thought for a moment and then pointed at *The Genie Handbook*. "Okay, book. Whatever. We mean what we said in the vow; we're up for the challenge and we won't tell anyone, not ever. So, come on, then—come on and make us genies!"

At once, the book began to shake. Skribble squawked and wriggled back down into his hole as the next page turned over by itself and almost flattened him. Sparks and specks of multicolored lights danced around *The Genie Handbook* like fireflies. The strange, unknowable squiggles on the ancient paper began to twist and unravel into proper words. . . .

"It believes us!" Milly gasped in excitement. "We're about to begin!"

The Genie Handbook

The First Step:
Finding Worthy Vessels

YOU WHO ARE WITNESS
TO THESE WORDS!

A genie is nothing without his lamp. A lamp is his vessel of conveyance, his home and hideaway. It is from here he bursts forth to greet his wish-maker with wondrous effect. It is also the repository of his magic, and wishes may go wrong if the lamp is not close by. As you are but a genie in training, this book will bind you and your lamp together with its magic, and enable you to grant wishes.

BUT FIRST! You must begin by finding a worthy vessel—or else let a worthy vessel find you. The lamp you choose should be pleasant to behold. It should exert a fascination over those who have magic in their hearts. An unhappy person should be compelled to pick up the lamp and rub it. For only in this way can a genie be summoned and commanded.

But before you embark on the first step, know this: Only worthy vessels are fit to hold great wisdom and knowledge. Whether you pass or fail, this test is in your hands, your heads—and your hearts. . . .

Chapter Four

"That seems to be it," said Jason, once he'd read it aloud. "The next page is just gibberish still." He turned back to the introduction and peered at the yellowed paper. "There *is* some small print after that first bit. 'Time turn. Time twist . . .'" He shook his head. "No, I can't read the rest. There's a big hole in the bottom of the page."

"I am *definitely* going to wake up in a minute," said Michael, who had closed his eyes.

"Did you notice the way the book talks about genies like they are all boys?" Jess pointed out. "'*His* lamp,' '*his* home and hideaway'—what about *girl* genies?"

"It's probably because it's an old book," Jason said. "So, it's just talking in an old-fashioned way."

"Plus," said Michael, opening one eye, "it's because boys are best."

Jess's eyes narrowed. "*What* did you say?"

Michael shrugged. "Boys happen to be the superior species, that's all."

"Ignore him," Milly advised her stepsister. "He's only trying to wind you up."

Jess smiled sweetly at Michael. "You can't be wound up by someone you don't take seriously."

"I bet you can be thumped by them, though!" Michael retorted.

"Anyway," said Jason, looking nervously between Jess and Michael. "The book says we have to find a lamp. How are we going to do that?"

"First we should start by making a list of good places to search." Jess began hunting around for some paper. "I'll be in charge and decide which of us looks where."

"Wait a second," said Michael. "Even if I really believed in any of this—and I'm not saying I do—why should *you* be in charge?"

"Because I'll be best at it," Jess said briskly.

"Yeah, right," he snorted. "Well, if there's any searching to be done, I reckon we should search in two teams, *proper* brothers and sisters—me and Milly against you and Jason."

"But I want to be on Jess's team!" Milly protested.

"Thanks, sis," said Michael sarcastically.

"I'll be on your team, Michael," Jason said.

"Okay." Jess squared up to Michael. "So it's girls against boys."

"Fine." Michael's eyes held hers. "Whoever finds the coolest lamp wins." He grabbed Jason by the collar and dragged him up the stairs. "Come on. Let's get looking, Jase."

"Yeah, get lost, you two," said Jess haughtily.

Milly nodded. "Jess and I are going to talk *tactics*."

"Tactics?" Michael looked a little uneasy. "What tactics?"

"Tactics. That's all." Milly gave Jess a knowing look, then smiled at him. "You'll see. . . ."

A few minutes later, Jason stood in Michael's room at the top of the house. Row upon row of shelves lined the walls, most of which were bare because Michael hadn't bothered to unpack his stuff yet.

"Do you think you've got a good lamp in here, then?" Jason asked.

"I think my brain's gone wrong and I'm seeing things that aren't there," said Michael. "Dad always said that video games would rot my mind, but I never believed him."

Jason considered this. "If the parietal lobes of your brain were damaged that could affect what you believe."

"I believe that you are a completely sad brainbox," said Michael, looking through some packing crates. "But forget this stupid so-called magic stuff for now. What really matters is that we thrash those girls at finding a lamp." He smiled to himself. "A lamp is just an old-fashioned flashlight, right? And I've got *loads* of flashlights."

"But is a flashlight really as good as a lamp?" Jason wondered.

"When we said the vow in old-fashioned words, it didn't work, did it? Not till I said it in modern talk." He nodded to himself. "So if we use a modern flashlight, this book you all believe in will be impressed, won't it? It'll think that we're using our heads. Aha!" He pulled out a white plastic tub and emptied out a load of flashlights in all shapes and sizes.

Jason spotted a problem. "How are we going to fit *inside* a flashlight?" he asked. "There's no room inside for a genie because of the batteries."

"Unless we use something like this!"

Jason stared as Michael held up what looked to be a rubber duck. If you squeezed the duck's sides, its bill lit up orange.

"The batteries are up its bum," Michael explained, holding the flashlight out to him. "So that means there'll be plenty of room in the wings and its stomach for a genie. What do you think?"

Jason took the flashlight and studied it. It was scuffed and dirty, and obviously hadn't been used for years. But the sides did squeeze—it went "quack" when you pressed them. "There's a squeaker in there, too," Jason said. "But I suppose there will be space around it."

"There we are then. Our magic genie lamp." Michael rubbed his hands together. "This competition's in the bag! Let's go downstairs and show the worm."

Jason hesitated. "Michael . . . the book said the lamp's supposed to be 'pleasant to behold.' That duck looks, well . . . like rubbish."

"If you're worried, we'll give it a wash." Michael spat on it and rubbed it under his armpit. "Come on, who's gonna rub a lamp these days and expect a genie to come out? No one, that's who. But who would find a duck flashlight and squeeze it to make it go 'quack'? *Loads* of people—if they're as crazy as we obviously are!" Michael flung open his bedroom door and scooted down the stairs. "Come on!"

"Wait for me!" Jason abandoned his doubts and bounded along behind him.

Chapter Five

"Okay," Jess said, looking at the notebook in her hand as she and Milly walked down the hill together, toward the town. "So we'll try Junk and Disorderly on East Street and see if we can find anything there."

"Cool!" Milly said, running down the hill. "Come on!"

Jess's thoughts were chasing their tails. *This whole genie-training thing can't be happening. But it is. But it can't be....* Her stomach was fizzing with nervous excitement, and she had to force herself to calm down, to concentrate on the normal, boring world around them.

It only made her more desperate to believe in magic.

As they approached the town center, the rows of houses gave way to shops. There were cafés with flowery curtains in the windows, gift shops selling china ornaments of shepherdesses and sheepdogs, and clothes shops with grubby plastic models that looked like they had been standing in the same place in the same clothes for the past twenty years.

"Look at this place," Jess sighed as they skirted past two old ladies in hats and tweed skirts. She thought about being back in London with coffee bars, music megastores, and Top Shop. "No one under the age of fifty would choose to live here."

"It's okay," said Milly. Then she started bouncing up and down. "Look, there's East Street!"

They turned down a cramped and cobbled street. The buildings on either side seemed to lean toward each other as if sharing secret gossip about the cyclists and pedestrians passing by. Junk and Disorderly was easy to spot. Its fading sign hung above a dark, dusty window packed full of old objects—brass figures, chipped ornaments, faded old pictures. Jess peered in through the grime. There was no one inside apart from a middle-aged man sitting behind the counter reading a battered paperback.

Jess felt slightly embarrassed about going inside the shop when it was empty, but Milly hurried straight in through the door.

The man looked up and smiled before turning back to his book, *1001 Quiz Questions*.

"Excuse me." Milly charged up to the counter and looked at the man brightly. "What's your name?"

The man frowned. "Barry."

"Well, Barry, I'm Milly and this is Jess, and we're look-ing for a lamp. An old lamp, like the kind that a genie could come out from."

Jess wanted to run out of the shop with embarrassment but Barry didn't seem at all taken aback. He smiled at Milly. "A lamp for a genie, eh? Is it for a school play?"

Milly nodded. "Sort of . . ."

"I think I might have just the thing," Barry said, leading the way toward the back of the shop. "How about this?" He took a dusty brass lamp off a high shelf. It had a round body and a long tall spout. The handle was twisted and had a snake's head rearing up at the end of it.

"Oh, wow!" Milly exclaimed. "It's perfect!" She took it from Barry and peered at the grimy patterns etched into the metal. Just beneath the spout was a jolly, extravagant figure in robes and a turban. "Look, Jess," she hissed. "There's even a genie on it."

Jess smiled as she took it. The lamp really *was* perfect.

Milly spun around to Barry. "How much is it?"

"Well, to most people, it would be ten pounds. . . ."

"Ten pounds!" Jess echoed.

"That's a *lot* of money," Milly said. She stared up at Barry, wide-eyed and tearful. "Our mum and dad have just moved here and they're really poor. It would be all our pocket money for a whole *month*. . . ."

"Milly!" Jess exclaimed, blushing at Milly's story.

But Barry just smiled. "Tell you what—you can have it for three pounds fifty, sweetheart."

The sadness vanished instantly from Milly's face. "Make it three pounds and you've got a deal!"

Barry laughed. "You're the biggest hustler I've ever had in here! All right. Three quid." He disappeared into the back of the shop. "I'll just go and wrap it up for you."

The doorbell jangled as two more people—a man and a woman—came into the shop. The man was tall and skinny with a razor-sharp moustache, smooth black hair, and dark eyes. The woman beside him was also tall and slender. Her black hair fell in a sleek bob and she had a parcel under her arm. They were both wearing suits and shiny shoes. Jess stared. They looked exotic and glamorous and not at all like the people she usually saw in Moreways Meet.

They approached the counter. Jess's skin prickled and she was gripped with a feeling of unease. Then the man looked straight at her. A shiver ran down Jess's spine as she met his gaze. She'd never seen such strange black eyes. They glittered like diamonds.

Contact lenses, she told herself. *He must have strange contact lenses in. No one has eyes like that.* Milly had noticed, too, and she took a step closer to Jess. It was like the shop had grown suddenly colder.

The man smiled at them both, very white teeth gleaming in his suntanned face.

Just then, Barry came bustling back with the lamp wrapped up in paper. "Here we are," he said, smiling at Milly.

Jess quickly paid him the money with trembling fingers. Then, with a quick "Thanks!" she and Milly marched past the strange-looking couple and out of the shop's battered door.

"Those people were really weird, weren't they?" Milly whispered. "Did you see their eyes?"

Jess nodded and glanced back into the shop. The woman was watching them through the window.

Jess was suddenly gripped with the urge to get as far away from the shop as possible. She didn't know why she felt so freaked out. She just did. "Come on," she said, grabbing Milly's arm. "Let's go!"

Michael pounded downstairs as if he was running a race. *This magic stuff can't be real,* he told himself. *And I'm gonna prove it when this dumb lamp thing doesn't work.* His heart was thumping and his hands felt sweaty as he clutched the duck flashlight. *Aren't I?*

He charged into the basement, Jason close behind.

The book was lying on the floor. Michael opened it, and Skribble popped up, looking as real and indignant as ever.

"What is it now?" he grumbled, spluttering bits of paper.

Jason frowned. "Are you eating the book?"

"And what if I am? What do you expect me to live on, stuck between these pages for two thousand years? Scotch mist? Babylonian fog?" Skribble fixed them with a beady look. "And what are you doing back here? You've been given a task; get on with it!"

"We *have* gotten on with it," Jason said excitedly.

Michael swallowed and held up the duck flashlight to show the bookworm. "Look!"

Skribble frowned so deeply that his face nearly folded in two. "What is *that*?"

Jason looked a bit crestfallen. "It's a flashlight."

"Foolish boys!" Skribble swayed from side to side like a cross little cobra. "You cannot get fire from a duck!"

"Not a *flaming* flashlight like you get in old castles," said Jason quickly. "A flashlight is like a lamp. It has batteries inside that power it."

"It's sort of a modern lamp," said Michael. He demonstrated by squeezing the plastic sides. The duck quacked and lit up.

Skribble shrank back in alarm.

"Me and Jase are modern blokes and this is a modern lamp," Michael declared. "And I'm dying to see what your precious book makes of it."

"Very well." Skribble looked at him closely, munching all the while. The words *fashion your fate* disappeared into the grave little stretch of his mouth. "Let us test your theory," he said. "Turn to the first step."

Michael quickly turned the pages back to the first step. This time, the gibberish was perfectly readable.

Jason sighed with relief. "That's got to be a good sign—hasn't it?"

Michael was astonished but determined not to show it. Had someone sneaked down here while they were away and rewritten the book? He read the words aloud:

> "*Once a worthy vessel has been found, the trainee genie can begin his lofty work by placing himself within the lamp. This he may do with the utterance of these simple words:*
> "'*GENIE ME!*'
> "*HOWEVER . . . take care and heed caution. Once inside, there the trainee genie must remain until summoned by whomsoever rubs the lamp. And from that moment on he is at the command*

of the wish-maker until the spell of release has been uttered."

"There you go!" Michael clapped Jason on the back. "Now we know how to get you in and out of there."

Jason blinked. "Me?"

"You're the big believer. . . ." Michael smirked. "Not *scared*, are you?"

"Um . . ." Jason swallowed hard. "No. Of course not."

"Well, go on then," Michael urged. "It's time we got this settled once and for all."

Jason looked at the duck flashlight in his hands. What else could he do? *"Genie me!"* he shouted.

And he vanished in a puff of red smoke.

The duck flashlight flopped to the floor, bounced once, and lay still.

Michael couldn't believe his eyes. He looked all around the den, half expecting to spot Jason hiding somewhere. A dizzy feeling swirled through him. Jase had disappeared. This was really happening! It really *was* magic!

"Hey!" called a muffled voice from down by his feet.

"Jason?" Michael's voice came out as a squeak. He stared around. "Where are you?"

"In the duck! It stinks of rubber, or plastic or something. And it's very squashed." A loud quack burst from the flashlight. "Ow!"

"No way!" Michael scooped up the plastic duck. "You must be, like, *really* small in there. Do you feel any different?"

"My head's stuck between my knees," said Jason. "It's not very comfy. Can you get me out?"

"Hang on. I'll give it a go." Michael gave the flashlight a gentle squeeze.

Nothing happened.

He rubbed it instead. Still nothing happened.

"Maybe I need to switch it on. . . ." He pressed both sides a little harder. With a further squeak, the bulb snapped on in the duck's bill.

"ARRRRRGH!" Jason shouted. "You squashed me and it got really hot and—OW! Turn it off!"

Michael bit his lip and squeezed again. Another quack, another cry from Jason, then the light went out. "Think," Michael told himself. "Think . . ." He tried rubbing the duck's head. No luck. Its tail. Nothing.

"Michael, are you still there?" Jason called. "Get me out."

"I can't," Michael whispered.

"Don't muck about, please—!"

"Jason, mate, I'm sorry!" Michael felt panic rising up inside him. "I never really believed I could get you in—and *I don't know how to get you out*!"

Chapter Six

"Noooooooo!" Jason's muffled wail floated eerily out of the flashlight. "I can't spend the rest of my life wedged inside a plastic duck! What about the spell of release the book talked about?"

"Brilliant!" Michael turned back to the book and reread what it said. "'. . . And from that moment on he or she is at the command of the wish-maker until the spell of release has been uttered.'" He closed his eyes and shook his head. "I don't believe it. It doesn't say what the spell of release is!"

"What?" Jason gasped. "Ask Skribble! Perhaps he can help."

"Perhaps? PERHAPS?" A familiar head popped up from the page. "Of course I can help! But why should I, hmm?"

"Please, Worm!" begged Michael.

Skribble's eyes narrowed. "I, help a miserable microbe who scarcely believes I am real? That *magic* is real?"

"I do believe it, I do," Michael gushed. "I guess I always did, but . . ." He sighed. "At my age, you're not supposed to believe in magic."

"I wish I did not have to believe in someone as stupid as you!" fussed Skribble. "But *I* do not doubt the evidence of my own eyes. A valuable lesson, boy, yes, very valuable."

"I'll pay you for it later," said Michael through gritted teeth. "Now, why can't I get Jason out?"

Skribble sighed. "What metal is that ridiculous contraption made from?"

Michael looked surprised. "It isn't metal. It's plastic."

"Exactly," Skribble said. "And just what is plastic, hmm?"

"A man-made material, made from polymers," Jason piped up from the duck. The squeaker gave a quiet wheeze.

Skribble shook his head and raised his voice. "You duck-brained dunces! The magic book knows nothing of your piffling plastics or polymers! Such substances did not exist when it was written."

Michael felt his heart sinking. "So the magic's only meant to work with metal?"

"And now it's gone wrong," Jason realized.

"How do we put things right?" Michael asked. "What's the release spell?"

"Oh, that's easy," said Skribble. "Child's play! You

47

simply say, 'Genie be free.'"

"Genie be free!" Michael shouted.

A belch of black smoke floated out of the duck's behind.

"Ooh!" said Jason. "That was like a shock going right through me."

"I must be on the right track," said Michael. He rubbed the duck and bellowed at the top of his lungs, "Genie be FREE!"

There was a flash of light, and the duck jumped out of Michael's grip. In a big cloud of smelly smoke, Jason suddenly appeared—all hunched up on the floor like he'd tried to curl himself into a ball.

"Jase!" Michael beamed. "I got you back! I did it!"

"I think you will find that *I* did it," Skribble pointed out.

"But what did you do?" gasped Jason, rocking on his knees. He was still all bunched up. "I can't move! I'm stuck in this stupid shape!"

Michael tried to straighten Jason's arms but they were as hard as stone. He tried again with his legs, but it was the same story.

"The magic's still not working properly," wailed Jason. "I'm stuck in the same shape as I was inside that duck. What if I stay this way forever?"

Michael groaned. "I'll be dead meat. Your mum will kill me! I'll be grounded forever!" He turned to Skribble. "Worm, you messed up! It didn't work."

"*I* messed up? I, indeed?" The bookworm vanished back inside the book with a cross jostling of pages. "*You* got yourselves into this mess. And as far as I'm concerned, you can stew in it!"

"I'm gonna squash that stupid worm," Michael growled, squeezing the tall, thin book into the back pocket of his jeans. "Guess I'd better get you out of sight before Dad and Ann see you." He took hold of Jason by the ankles and hauled him over to the staircase. "It's okay, Jase; we'll think of something. We will!"

He felt the book vibrate in his back pocket, like something small and smug was laughing.

A little while later, Milly and Jess arrived back home and raced up the stairs. "Just wait till we show the boys the lamp!" Milly exclaimed. "Come on!"

Jess followed her up to the landing. "Oh, stupid boy looo-sers . . ." she called.

Michael opened his bedroom door a little and stuck his head out. He looked pale. "Come in, guys!" he hissed. "Quick!"

Milly and Jess hurried into the room. At the same

moment, they stopped dead and gasped.

"Jason!" Milly exclaimed in horror.

Jason groaned. His back was aching and all his muscles felt stiff. "Magic . . . went wrong . . ."

Jess swung around furiously toward Michael. "What have you done to him?"

As Michael explained what had happened, Milly's and Jess's eyes grew wider and wider.

"Oh, Jase!" breathed Milly, dropping her parcel and flinging her arms around him.

"There must be something we can do to *un*magic him," said Jess, feeling close to tears.

"Oh, Skribble, can you help us?" Milly asked, crouching down beside the book on the floor. "Oh, please, please do. You're so clever. . . ."

There was a rustling sound as Skribble popped out of *The Genie Handbook.* "At last," he said, preening himself. "Someone is talking sense."

"You'll help us?" Jess asked breathlessly.

"Well, I *suppose* I could. . . ."

"You didn't say that when I asked you!" Michael exclaimed.

Skribble fixed him with a beady stare. "Maybe *you* didn't ask properly!"

"We've got a lamp! We found it in a junk shop in town."

Milly unwrapped her parcel. "Here it is!"

Scribble's neck moved from side to side as he examined the lamp. "Early fourteenth century by the look of things," he said approvingly. "Well-wrought metal. Yes, it might just do. . . ."

"How do we use it to help Jason?" Jess demanded. Skribble raised his tiny eyebrows, and Jess hastily adjusted her words. "I mean, please would you be so kind as to tell us how to help Jason, clever Skribble?"

Skribble looked pleased. "Very well. Firstly, one of you must invoke the powers of mortal-to-genie trans-mogrification."

Milly stared. "Do what?"

"Say, 'Genie me!'" Jason translated. "It puts you inside the lamp."

"Then, the trainee genie must be conjured out by another rubbing the lamp," Skribble went on. "The genie will be able to grant a wish restoring this unfortunate boy to his usual state."

"Okay." Jess looked at the lamp and hesitated. "Um . . . would you like to do it, Milly?"

"Yes, please!" Milly said eagerly.

"You're only letting Milly do it because *you* don't want to!" Michael protested.

"You do it, then!" Jess snapped back.

Michael went red. "Well," he mumbled. "I guess if Milly really *wants* to go in there . . ."

"I do," said Milly firmly. "I *must*." She glanced at Jason, twisted into such a horrible shape. He looked so unhappy, but tried to give her a reassuring smile.

She glanced at Skribble. He nodded his little head encouragingly.

It's now or never! thought Milly, holding the lamp tight.

"Genie me!" she cried.

Chapter Seven

There was a bright white flash and the next second the world seemed to turn upside down. Milly felt herself spinning around as if she were on the teacups ride at the fair. "Whoaaaa!" she cried.

Her voice echoed back at her with a metallic ring.

Milly blinked her eyes open. She was standing in a very dark, very musty place. She reached out and touched a wall on her left. It felt cold and as if it was made of metal. Groping blindly in the darkness, she stepped to the right. After a few paces, her outstretched fingers touched another curved metal wall.

I'm in the lamp, she realized. Her brain reeled. She shivered, feeling suddenly very alone.

She became aware of warmth filling the lamp. "Someone's rubbing it!" She didn't know how she knew that was what was happening; she just did. Suddenly, feeling as if she was being sucked up by a giant vacuum cleaner, Milly was pulled upward through the spout.

"Wooooo!" she cried as she somersaulted through the air and ended up her normal size, standing on the carpet in Michael's room.

Jess, Michael, and Jason all stared at her.

Milly stared back at them, just as amazed as they were.

Then Michael started to grin. "Cool outfit, Mil!"

"What . . . ?" Milly looked down. Her jeans and sneakers had been replaced by baggy gold trousers and a pair of red shoes with toes that went up at the end. Her T-shirt had turned into a strappy gold-and-red top. She twitched her mouth. She had a strange feeling, as if there was something bristly there. Her hands flew to her top lip and felt a thick carpet of hairs curving out at either side of her nose and curling upward.

Michael sniggered. Jess began to giggle. Even Jason, despite his predicament, looked like he was trying not to laugh.

"I . . . I've got a moustache!" Milly exclaimed.

Skribble frowned. "Well, of course you have. That's the way a genie should look, according to humans." Milly looked at him blankly. "You can't choose what you look like until Step Two of the training. Then you'll learn how to change your appearance to suit yourself." He sighed disapprovingly as he looked at Michael and Jess, who were now clutching their sides and choking with laughter. "*If you get that far!*"

Milly glared at Jess and Michael. "It's not that funny."

"Oh, believe me, it is!" Michael gasped.

"Stop laughing at me!" Milly told them furiously. "Or I'll go back into the lamp and stay there!"

"You can't do that," said Skribble. "No going back into the lamp in Step One until you grant a wish, or attempt to grant one, at the very least. Those are genie training rules. At the moment, you are under the command of the older girl. Whatever she tells you to do, you must try to perform it."

Milly turned to her stepsister in alarm. "Jess! I don't like this!"

Jess wiped her eyes. "Sorry, Milly." She took a deep breath and tried to control herself. "I'll make the wish. . . . I wish that Jason was back to normal!"

For a fleeting second, Milly wondered how she could make the wish come true. But then *The Genie Handbook* started to shake on the floor, and suddenly her body seemed to act of its own accord. She felt a tingling sensation run through her from the top of her head to the tips of her toes. Her hands lifted into the air and her mouth jerked open as the words seemed to jump from her throat:

"Your wish is my command!" Her voice boomed out as if she was speaking through a microphone. Then there was a bright silver flash.

Milly blinked. As she opened her eyes, she saw the others blinking too, the laughter gone from their faces.

And suddenly, there was Jason, back to normal! He stretched out his arms and legs, and wiggled his fingers. "You did it, Milly! Oh, thank you, you did it!"

"Wow!" Milly breathed. "I really did, didn't I! Just think what else I could do. . . ."

"You have done quite enough for the time being," said Skribble. "Now you must return to the lamp."

Milly pouted. "Must I?"

Skribble nodded. "Picture yourself back inside the lamp in your mind. Your body will follow."

Reluctantly, Milly did as he said. Soon, she felt the sucking sensation just as before—and found herself pulled back into the lamp! She had barely gathered her wits before she heard Jess's voice, as if from far, far away. . . .

"Genie be free!"

Like a cork popping from a bottle, Milly shot out of the lamp and landed on the carpet, only this time she landed in a heap and her clothes were back to normal. She felt weak and her head was spinning. "What happened?" she gasped, her hands reaching up to her face.

There was no moustache!

"You have been released from the lamp, of course," Skribble explained. "I divulged the phrase that would set you free to your sister—"

"Stepsister," said Jess automatically.

Skribble bristled. "Whatever the piffling distinctions . . . Milly, you are no longer under her command."

"And you look normal again!" Jess added.

Milly grinned at her. It was the nicest thing anyone had ever said to her.

"I'm normal again, too!" shouted Jason, running around the room, stretching and putting himself into funny ballet-style poses. "Look at me!"

"No, thanks," said Michael. But then he clapped Jason on the shoulder. "Glad to have you back."

"Thanks," said Jason, with a grateful look at Milly. "If it hadn't been for you and Skribble . . ."

"That's okay," said Milly. "But I wish I could have done more magic."

"That is how all students feel the first time they grant a wish," Skribble informed her. "But never forget, any of you, that you are students learning a serious craft—not infants playing games. The secrets of the book are not imparted lightly." He looked sternly at each of them in turn. "Do you all understand?"

The children nodded. "Sorry, Skribble," Milly murmured.

The bookworm's face softened. "Do not worry, my dear. You did very well."

"And I guess the important thing is, you found a cool lamp," said Michael quietly. "Fair play. You won."

Jess nodded. "Girls are best!"

"At being annoying," Michael conceded.

Jason was looking through the pages of the book. Everything after the first step was still in a mysterious language. He sighed. "We might have a lamp now but we still haven't passed Step One. I guess we shouldn't have used that duck flashlight, Michael. We should have thought about it more."

Michael grunted. "I messed up. I think deep down, I didn't believe anything magic would really happen, so it didn't matter."

"But it *does* matter," said Jason.

Milly nodded fervently. "It matters more than anything."

"I think we should *all* agree to be more careful in the future," Jess said.

Suddenly, Skribble gasped. "There's something happening in the book! My tail's tingling! The words are changing."

Jess bit her lip. "Maybe it's going to let us pass to the next step after all!"

Milly crossed all her fingers. "Oh, please, oh, please, oh, please!"

Strange lights and patterns seemed to flick over the yellowed paper. "Turn the page!" Skribble ordered.

Jason quickly flicked the page over and found that the words had turned into English. "I can read it!" he exclaimed. "We *have* passed on to Step Two!"

"Read out what it says," said Milly.

So, Jason picked up the book and began to read. . . .

The Genie Handbook

The Second Step:
Worlds of Change and Appearance

YOU WHO ARE WITNESS
TO THESE WORDS!

You have overcome your first challenge and learned the valuable lesson that only fools rush in where wise men fear to tread. But now your wisdom and judgment will be tested further. As a genie, you must be able to bend and break the nature of reality in order to satisfy a wishmaker's heart's desire.

BUT FIRST! You will need to cloak your form in the magical guise of geniedom. Trainees must NOT be recognized by those they perform magic upon. You must be impressive. You must command respect.

Once you have mastered the art of disguising yourself, you may work to disguise the true appearance of THINGS.

However—HEED THESE WORDS! A wise

genie will proceed gently as he learns the arts of transformation. Be vigilant. Be ever observant. If you strive to see through an object's outward form, you may find a truth at its heart.

Chapter Eight

"See through the outward form," Michael mused. "I've always fancied X-ray vision."

"I don't think it means *really* look through the outward form," said Jess.

"But what *does* it mean?" said Milly.

"Dinner's ready!" Ann Worthington called up the stairs.

Milly's face crumpled in disappointment. "We can't have dinner now!"

"Not hungry!" Michael yelled.

"Tough!" his stepmum shouted back.

"We'd better go," said Jason quickly. "We can come straight back afterward."

"I wouldn't bother," said Skribble sniffily. "I have helped you far too much already today, and I am extremely tired. We shall begin again at sunrise."

"Sunrise?" Michael nearly choked. "That's, like . . . *early*!"

"Time is of the essence, boy!" said Skribble. "Come

back first thing in the morning. There is much to be done."
He wriggled back inside the book.

"I'M NOT TELLING YOU LOT AGAIN!" shouted
Ann Worthington. "DINNER—*NOW!*"

"Coming!" called Jason quickly.

Michael sighed. "Suppose we'd better get down there
before your mother grounds us."

"Mum's never grounded *me* in my life," Jess informed
him.

"That's 'cause you're so boring you never go out anyway," he shot back.

Milly rolled her eyes at Jason. "There they go again," she
sighed as Michael and Jess went downstairs bickering.

"If they mess with Mum when she's in a mood like
this, they're history!" said Jason. "And we will be, too.
Come on!"

"Hang on! What about the book?" Milly pointed out.
"We can't just leave it here in Michael's room; it'll get
buried under rubbish and Skribble won't like that. Should
I hide it under my pillow?"

Jason nodded and they hurried down the stairs, stopping briefly in Milly and Jess's bedroom.

"See you later, Skribble," Milly whispered, stroking the
book as she tucked it safely inside her pillowcase.

"Hurry up!" Jason urged her.

They charged the rest of the way to the kitchen, catching up with Jess and Michael at the door. There were three large, slightly soggy pizzas on the table. Mark was putting out plates and Ann was shaking some limp salad from a bag into a bowl.

"Pizza again," Jess sighed. They'd had pizza for the last three nights.

"I think even I am reaching my frozen pizza limit," said Michael.

"Tough," said Ann.

"You can never have too much pizza, that's what I say," Mark said quickly, sitting next to him. "Pass the meat feast, Michael."

As Michael pushed one of the pizzas along the table, Ann brought the bowl of salad over. "Of course, if you feel like preparing a home-cooked meal for the whole family, kids, then don't let me stop you." She put the bowl down with a slight bang.

Jess saw the look of tiredness on her face and felt bad. Her mum and Mark had been working so hard in their new shop that it was no wonder they hadn't had time to cook anything else. She got up and helped give out the salad. "So what have you been doing today, Mum?"

"We sorted through some stock here," Ann replied. "Then I went into town and bought a couple of ornaments for the shop from Junk and Disorderly."

"We went there!" Milly piped up. Then she yelped as Michael kicked her under the table. "I mean . . . in a game, we did. I played the part of the shopkeeper. I improvised."

"You and your acting, Milly," Ann said, smiling at her and not suspecting a thing. Michael, Jess, and Jason breathed a sigh of relief.

"So how's everything going at the shop?" Jess asked.

Ann pushed her hair back from her face. "There's still an awful lot to do. I can't believe we're opening in a week's time. I shouldn't have wasted my time going around junk shops. . . ."

"You needed a break," said Mark supportively. "Hey, maybe you kids could all help out tomorrow morning? A lot of the books need putting on shelves, and—"

"No!" The word burst out of Milly before she could stop herself.

Her dad frowned. "Why not?"

"That sounds like a great idea," Jess said smoothly. "We'd all *love* to help. Wouldn't we?" She looked sharply around at the others.

"Oh, yeah," Michael muttered, pushing away his half-eaten plate of pizza. "It would be the biggest thrill of my life."

* * *

"Why did you say we'd help in the shop tomorrow?" Milly hissed to Jess as soon as they left the table and were out of earshot. "You *know* we're supposed to be starting Step Two of *The Genie Handbook*."

"I *had* to say it." Jess led the way down to the den. "We don't want Mum and Mark to think something strange is going on or they'll be watching us all the time. *This* way, if we help out in the morning it'll get them off our backs, and then we'll have the afternoon to do Step Two."

"Cool," said Milly happily. "I can't believe we're actually learning to be genies! What are you going to wish for when we can have wishes, Jase?"

Jason's mind spun with the possibilities. "I dunno."

"And whose wish will we grant first?" Jess said.

"Mine," Michael suggested.

Milly rolled her eyes. "Shut up!"

Jess considered the question. "Maybe it might be a good idea if we all make a list of the top five wishes we want to have. Then we can see if we can agree on any."

Jason nodded. "That's a good idea. We could grant those wishes first."

"Okay," the others agreed.

"Let's do them now!" said Milly. "Come on, Jess!"

The boys went off, and Jess followed Milly into their shared room.

On Milly's side, the wooden floor was covered with cuddly toys, animal magazines, and piles of discarded clothes. The duvet was half off the bed and the chest of drawers was covered in a jumble of photos of friends and tiny ornaments.

Jess's side, on the other hand, was a perfect picture of neatness. Her plain white duvet was smooth and unruffled, the pillows plumped up. On top of her chest of drawers her hairbrush, hair straightener, and bits of makeup were lined up in rows. She had a desk and CD rack with her CDs arranged in alphabetical order, and on her bedside table there was a magazine and a single photo frame with a picture of her two best friends from London.

Jess opened the top drawer of her desk and took out a notebook. She sat down on the chair and began to think. *What am I going to wish for?*

Grabbing a piece of paper and a felt-tip pen, Milly jumped onto Jess's bed. "What are your wishes going to be, Jess?"

"I don't know yet. Oh, Milly, go to your own bed," Jess said crossly. "You're creasing my duvet!"

Milly rolled her eyes and went back to her own side of the room. She sat on the bed and put her hand under her pillow. She could feel the book in her pillowcase. It felt warm and her fingers tingled slightly. Excitement fizzed through her. They could have real wishes! What would her top five be?

She thought for a moment and then began scribbling down her list:

1. Go back to London and be Dorothy
2. Have a pony
3. Have a dog
4. Be a famous actress
5. Have lots and lots of money

Other stuff flew through her mind. There were so many wishes that would be cool—being able to fly, having an animal sanctuary, being able to read people's thoughts, being a ballerina or a movie star or both! She sighed. It was impossible. How could she *ever* choose just five things?

On the other side of the room, Jess had written her number one wish very neatly into her notebook:

1. Go back to London

Her pen hovered over the page as she wondered what exactly she meant by that. Did she want them to go back to their old houses and be two separate families again? Or did she mean she wanted them to live in one big house together? She chewed a fingernail and considered it.

She liked Mark, and she knew her mum was happy with him. But did they really all have to live together? Milly was so noisy and messy. And Michael was *really* annoying. Whenever she went into the bathroom there was always a pair of pants or socks on the floor. He left his bath towel in a wet heap and he *always* left the toilet seat up!

She began to add in some more details to her wish list:

1. *To go back to London and live in our old houses in our own rooms and go to our old schools again, but Mum and Mark could still see each other.*
2. *To have a million pounds*
3. *To have a nicer nose*
4. *To have a boyfriend . . .*

She suddenly stopped writing as she remembered that they were going to be showing their lists to each other. She ripped the page out. There was no way she could show Michael those last two wishes! She decided to play it safe:

3. *To go on holiday to a tropical island*

*4. To go to Hollywood and see any celebrities
I want
5. To be allowed to stay out as late as I want to
whenever I want to*

There, she thought, reading down her list. *My five
wishes.*

Upstairs, the boys were writing their own lists. Jason was
typing his wishes on the family computer on the landing.

1. I wish for world peace.
2. To go into space
3. To have an unlimited supply of chocolate
4. To be on TV

He thought for a moment. He knew the others really
wanted to go back to London. *Do I want to?* he wondered. It would be good to see his old friends. But he
liked his new school, too. He'd only been there for two
weeks before the Easter holidays had started, but his
classmates were okay and there was a computer club
and a science club he wanted to join when they went
back after the holidays. . . .

But then, Jess was so unhappy in Moreways Meet, and Michael was too, and Milly wanted to be Dorothy. . . . And it *would* be good to be back with his friends. He made up his mind and decisively typed:

5.   Go back to London

Just then, Mark came along the corridor. Jason hastily closed the document.

"Doing homework, mate?" Mark asked.

Jason nodded.

Mark smiled. "Wish Michael was more like you." He patted Jason rather awkwardly on the back. "Keep up the good work. I'll . . . er, catch you later."

Jason watched him go. He knew Mark thought it was odd that he was so quiet and was into math, science, and computers. But he really liked his stepdad. He opened up his list again and deleted his fourth wish, changing it to:

4.   To make Mum and Mark stop arguing and be happy

He looked through his list and then nodded. *Yes,* he thought, *those are the things I would like to wish for most.*

In his room on the top floor, Michael had scrawled his list very quickly:

1. Go back to London
2. Have never-ending cash supplies
3. Have X-ray vision and see through anything
4. Have mind control
5. Have the power to travel anywhere in the world in two seconds

Now he lay back on his bed, his hands behind his head. What would be the first thing he bought with his endless cash? The new Megaplay Ultra, he decided, thinking of the latest game console to hit the market. And then an iPhone, a new mega-cool stereo, of course, a wide-screen plasma TV for his room, and then . . .

Lost in happy thoughts, he sighed and grinned. Maybe believing in magic was okay after all!

Chapter Nine

The next morning everyone trooped down to the book-shop after breakfast. Jason helped Mark put up some shelves while Jess set to work arranging a pile of books in alphabetical order, and Milly "improved" the children's area by sticking beads and sequins on the sides of the girl's fiction shelves.

Michael had to clean some grotty old bookcase with Ann. He pulled out a pile of books from the bottom shelf and put them on top, accidentally knocking over a funny-looking brass vase with a narrow neck.

"Careful," said Ann. "It may have come from a junk shop but it's not junk!"

"Sorry," Michael muttered. "My arm aches."

"I thought you'd have big muscles from all that computer game playing," said Ann lightly.

Michael snorted. "They're video games."

She smiled at him. "I really do appreciate your help-ing us, Michael. You see, it's not *that* bad when we all do something together as a family, is it?"

"Guess not." Michael felt a twinge of guilt as he remembered the number one wish on the piece of paper stuffed into his pocket. He and the others had agreed to compare their lists on the way back from the shop.

At lunchtime, Mark decided to let his slave labor force go free.

"There's cold pizza in the fridge for lunch!" called Ann as they left the shop.

"Oh, great," Jess muttered. "*More* pizza."

"So, what's on everyone's lists?" Milly burst out as soon as they were a few shops away. She pulled her own list out of her pocket. "Can I tell you mine first? Please?"

"Okay," said Jess.

Milly gabbled out what she had written. "What did you all put?" she asked when she'd finished.

They each read out their lists.

"Looks like we'll be wishing to go back to London, then," Jess said with a satisfied smile. "After all, it's the only wish that's on *all* our lists!"

"And we'll be going back with loads of cash!" said Michael, rubbing his hands together. "How cool is that?"

"But first we have to pass another five steps of the handbook," Jason pointed out.

"No problem!" said Michael. "We'll ace them all!"

"Come on!" Milly said eagerly. "Let's get back and see Skribble!"

"What time do you call this?" Skribble exclaimed, popping out of *The Genie Handbook*'s pages as they came into the den, his face a florid shade of pink. "I told you to consult me at sunrise. It is now well after noon! What do you mean by this tardiness? Explain yourselves!"

"Calm down, Worm!" Michael said. "We had to help my dad and Ann down at the shop!"

"Shop? *Shop?*" Skribble shook with fury. "I offer to share with you my vast experience and infinite wisdom, to waste my precious time helping you to make your heart's desire come true, and do you embrace my kind self-sacrifice? No! You go merrily off to some silly *shop*, if you please!"

"I'm sorry, Skribble," said Milly. "We wanted to come and see you, really we did. But we have to do what our parents tell us to, or we'll get in real trouble."

"Real trouble, she says!" Skribble shook his head. "Oh, my dear girl, you don't know the meaning of those words." A shiver seemed to run through the bookworm's whole body.

Jason looked at him curiously. "What do you mean, Skribble?"

"Nothing," said the bookworm quickly.

Suddenly, Jess gasped. She had just noticed something about the book. "This picture wasn't here yesterday, I'm sure!" She pointed to a picture of a lamp. "It looks like ours. . . ." Then she turned back a few pages and gasped. "Look! There are pictures of *us*!"

She held the book out and the others stared. Pictures had appeared before the beginning of Step Two. The first showed Jess and Milly holding the lamp in the junk shop. There was a caption written underneath it in indigo ink.

" 'Careful planning reaps rewards,' " Milly read out.

"What *is* this?" Jess breathed. "I mean . . . that's us! And the detail, it's spot-on."

"Of course it is!" Skribble tutted. "The book is summing up your progress, what you did well . . ." He fixed Michael with a pointed look. "And what you did very *badly*."

"Hey! Look at this one!" said Milly, pointing out a picture of Jason doubled over. "That's when you came out of the duck flashlight."

" 'Only a fool takes magic lightly,' " Michael read out. He turned the page to find a picture of Milly bursting out of the lamp, her moustache flapping wildly. "Hey, good likeness, Mil!"

Milly read the caption scrawled beneath: " 'Working together will benefit all.' "

"It's like the book's saying why it passed us," said Jason, staring at the pictures.

"Indeed it is," said Skribble. "The book will judge you all at the end of each step, deciding if you deserve to go on with your training."

"It's so weird to think it's watching us," said Jess with a shudder.

"Well, enough of this time wasting," Skribble announced. "To business!" He nodded toward the genie lamp that sat on top of the dresser. "You have all read the introduction to Step Two. The book now requires you to learn about the worlds of appearance and illusion. Begin by taking turns to get in and out of the lamp as impressively as possible, disguising your appearance in whatever way you see fit."

"Why don't you give it a go, Jess?" said Milly, passing her the lamp. "It's amazing in there. You're so small, but you feel really big."

Jess took a deep breath. *"Genie me!"* she commanded.

One second she was there, the next she had gone. Vanished. And the lamp was lying on the floor.

Milly picked up the lamp and rubbed it. Jess burst out in a cloud of pink smoke, arms folded across her chest. She was wearing a pale green turban, a glittering red top with a mauve veil, and ultramarine baggy trousers, which clashed horribly.

"Nice outfit," Michael smirked. "You're, like, the thrift shop genie."

"Shut up!" Jess boomed in a deep, thunderous voice that made the windows rattle.

"Very good voice!" said Skribble, nodding his approval. "Yes, that *is* a voice that will command respect."

"It'll deafen people!" cried Jason. "Turn it down, Jess!"

"All right," Jess said, a little more quietly. She felt her top lip. "Phew! I'm glad I haven't got a moustache." She looked down at her weird clothes and sighed. "But this outfit *is* horrible. I hoped I'd come out in something cool."

"Hope! You can't just *hope*, girl!" Skribble exclaimed. "You must use your imagination and picture what your disguise will be!"

"Well, it's someone else's turn now," Jess said. "How do I get back inside the lamp?"

"As I told Milly," said Skribble, "simply place yourself there in your mind, and your body will follow."

Jess closed her eyes and imagined herself within those musty, metal walls. In the blink of an eye she had vanished back into the lamp.

"Genie be free!" Milly commanded. As Jess appeared

beside her, back to normal if a little shell-shocked, Milly turned to her brother. "Michael, do you want a turn?"

"Um . . ." Michael looked at Jason. "I think you should go first, mate."

When Jason appeared, he came out in a gust of brown smoke with the sound of a colossal fart.

Milly giggled. "Jason!"

"You cannot emerge making a noise like that, boy!" said Skribble firmly. "You will be a laughingstock!"

"I—I didn't mean to," said Jason, looking mortified. He was dressed in a green silk suit with funny slippers that curled up at the end, and a moustache to match. His turban was white and perfectly folded. "It just sort of came out."

"Wasn't a total disaster, though, Jase," said Michael. "Fair play—that's awesome face fuzz."

"Really?" Jason peered into the bedside mirror at his moustache. "Hey! It is quite good, isn't it? I wasn't even thinking of a moustache, either."

"Must be natural skill," said Milly, pleased for him.

"Natural stupidity, more like," said Skribble disdainfully. "That, my beetle-brained boy, is a *default* moustache. The lamp chose it for you." He tutted. "Really, if you wish to pass this step, you will have to display more imagination. A very good deal more!"

"I *do* want to pass," said Jason earnestly. "I really do."

Skribble sniffed. "Back in the lamp with you."

Jason held his nose and closed his eyes—and was sucked up inside the lamp like dust into a vacuum cleaner. Milly set him free and he popped back into reality, looking normal once more.

"Now then," said Skribble. "You—older boy."

"Michael," said Michael indignantly.

"Yes, whatever your name is. It is high time you stopped laughing at the others and took a turn yourself."

"Right. Cool. Whatever." Michael frowned and bit his lip. "Not a problem."

Milly squeezed her brother's hand supportively. "Hey. It's okay to be scared," she said quietly. Then she pinched him and laughed. "Don't feel dumb and useless just because your little sister did it easy as anything!"

"*And* your stepsister," Jess teased him. "And your little stepbrother . . ."

"I'm not little!" said Jason, turning up his nose. "And Michael's not scared of anything. Are you, Michael?"

Michael scowled at the girls, and looked at the lamp in Jason's hands. "Genie me!" he snapped.

The book shook and Michael felt himself whizzing away like water down a drain. He whooped—it was like the most excellent fairground ride you could ever imagine.

Suddenly, everything was dark around him, and Michael could taste the tang of old metal at the back of his throat. "Did it!" he whispered. "Now to show them what a *real* genie looks like . . ."

He concentrated hard, and the next moment heard the squeak of fingertips on metal. Michael felt his whole body fizz like a shaken-up can of soda. . . .

WHOOOSH! He shot out of the lamp spout so fast he banged his head on the ceiling. "Ow!" he boomed, and landed in a heap on the floor.

"Wow, Michael," said Jason. "You look cool!"

"More like crazy!" said Milly.

Michael got up and marveled at his reflection. Just as he'd pictured in his mind, he was wearing a silk ninja-style outfit, the black material bisected by a golden sash. His turban was black too, with a huge glowing ruby in its center. "Hey, check the beard!" he cried. It was enormous and bushy and came down to his diamond-covered slippers.

"You look totally dumb," said Jess with some pleasure.

"What would you know?" Michael tossed the beard over his shoulder. "I could trap badgers in this."

"You could tie it around your waist and use it as a belt!" said Jason, trying to join in. Michael ignored him.

"Is it a real beard?" Milly wondered, and yanked on it hard.

"Ow!" Michael yelped. "Yes, it is!"

Milly grinned. "My turn now!"

Michael imagined himself back into the lamp and Jason set him free.

"Now then, Milly," said Skribble, a slightly softer edge to his voice. "Into the lamp you go. But don't forget to really *use* your imagination."

Jason passed Milly the lamp. "Knock on the inside when you're ready to come out."

Milly nodded and slipped both hands around it, tracing its swirling, tarnished patterns with her fingers. "Genie me!" she whispered.

And with a now familiar WHOOSH, she was drawn inside.

Finding herself inside the lamp, Milly thought hard. What did she want to look like? Blue trousers, she decided, a glittering peacock blue. She imagined herself wearing those with a silver top that just showed off her tummy. And she wanted a turban—a red one with a big emerald in the center. That just left her face. *No moustache,* she thought firmly. *No beard, either.* Shutting her eyes, she imagined herself until the image was so real she felt as if she could reach out and touch the genie Milly.

Now! she thought.

She rapped quickly on the inside of the lamp. There was the familiar warm swirling sensation. *Jess must be rubbing the side,* she realized, but no sooner than the thought had formed, she found herself shooting upward. She burst out of the lamp in a shower of silver sparks.

"Hey!" she gasped, landing on the carpet and holding out her arms.

"You look great, Milly!" Jess exclaimed, with a tinge of envy.

Milly went to the mirror. She looked just like she'd imagined herself—only better. The trousers were embroidered with silver thread and the material glittered and shone, her silver top sparkled, and the emerald in her turban glowed. Best of all, she had no moustache! "Cool," she breathed.

Skribble nodded in approval. "May I say what a delightful genie you make, Milly."

"And may *I* say, I'm starving," said Michael grumpily. "It's way past lunchtime."

Milly frowned. "How can you think about food? We're doing magic!"

"Even trainee genies need to eat," said Michael. "Come on, sis, change back."

"But there is still much to do," Skribble protested. "You

all need to try harder! You must practice, over and over!"

"Maybe we'll do better on a full stomach," said Jess. "We can practice again after we've eaten."

Milly sighed, shut her eyes, and whizzed back into the lamp. She heard Jess say, "Genie be free!" Then she popped out of the spout, full-size again. Michael and Jason were already leaving the room. Jess put the lamp down on her bed, and followed them out. Skribble was left looking quite forlorn, his head peeping from the book.

"We'll be back soon, Skribble," Milly said, looking into his little eyes. "Thank you for helping me with my genie look!"

The worm looked pleased. "Yes, well . . . hurry back quickly, my dear. There is no time to be complacent!"

Milly grinned and ran downstairs after Jess and the others. She found them in the kitchen looking in the fridge.

"I really can't face pizza again," Jess sighed. "I think I'll just make myself a sandwich."

Milly looked at the rock-hard remains of a loaf on the breadboard. "With that? You'll need a chain saw to cut through it."

"There are some old baked beans and a bit of cheese in the fridge," Jason observed. "We could use our imaginations and do something with them."

"Better than doing something with this." Michael weighed the half loaf in both hands. "This isn't food anymore; it's an offensive weapon." As if to prove his point, he dropped it on Jason's foot.

"Ow!" Jason started hopping around the room. Jess gave Michael a cross shove. Michael gave her one back.

"You're right, Jase!" Milly said suddenly.

"What about?" said Jason, still clutching his toes.

"It's like you said—we should use our imaginations. Worlds of appearance and change!"

Jason stopped hopping as he realized what she meant. "You mean we could use magic?" He pulled the cheddar out of the fridge. "We could change this old cheese and the bread—"

"Into a delicious mega-feast!" Milly nodded quickly.

"That's actually a cool idea," said Michael, looking impressed.

"Brilliant!" said Jess. "We could have proper food for a change."

"Do you think we're allowed to use magic for that?" said Jason.

Milly ran to the door. "Let's get the book and ask Skribble—now!"

Chapter Ten

illy and Jason ran upstairs to see Skribble and explain their idea. The little bookworm seemed to approve.

"Not a bad test of your abilities, I suppose," he said. "It may give you food for thought, at any rate!"

"We can make whatever we like," said Milly. Jason grabbed the lamp and she carefully picked up the book. "Come on!"

"Not too quickly!" Skribble commanded. "I get airsick."

They came back downstairs to find Michael and Jess had laid out four empty plates on the kitchen table. Milly put Skribble and the book down on the kitchen counter.

"Right then, Worm," said Michael. "How can we make a tasty all-you-can-eat grub marathon out of some cold baked beans, a bit of moldy cheddar, and some rock-hard bread?"

"Since you have a rock-hard *head* as well, I'm not

entirely sure you can," said Skribble. "Who intends to be the genie?"

"Let me try again!" Jess said eagerly. "Genie me!" she gasped as she was tugged down into the lamp, then tried to collect her thoughts while she waited for Jason to summon her. Yes, she knew how she wanted to appear. . . .

There was a fizzing feeling in her tummy as the lamp began to shake. Jess shot out through the spout, looking stunning in a gold miniskirt, glittering gold boots, and a gold cutoff top. She had a diamond in her belly button and a delicate diamond-and-gold tiara on her head.

"That's a brilliant outfit!" Milly declared.

"Thanks." Jess smiled. "I just really pictured in my head what I wanted to look like. . . ."

Michael yawned noisily. "How about granting a wish sometime this year?"

"Jess, for my lunch, I wish I had a huge plate of sausage and mash, please," Jason burbled. "With gravy!"

Jess drew herself up to her full height. "Your wish is my . . ." She frowned. "How do I do it?"

"Transform that bit of cheese," said Michael, tipping it out onto one of the empty plates on the kitchen table.

"Picture it in your head," Milly advised. "That's what I did when I unfroze Jase."

Sausages, Jess thought to herself, imagining them

sizzling in a pan. *Sausages and fluffy mashed potatoes with no lumps* . . . She pictured a big plateful of mash, neatly ringed with sausages, and then smothered the whole lot with deep brown gravy. For good measure, she imagined four frankfurters sticking out of the whippy potatos like birthday candles.

The book on the floor trembled. Jess's hands shot up. "Your wish is my command!" she boomed, her genie voice echoing around the room.

A flash of gold lit up the air. Everyone gasped as a plate of sausages and mash appeared!

"Oh, wow!" Jess laughed out loud with delight. "I did it! I just did *real* magic!"

"It looks amazing!" Michael grinned, too, and slapped a knife and fork into Jason's hand. "Dig in, then, Jase!"

Jason speared one of the sausages and scooped up a huge forkful of mash with it. But as he stuck it in his mouth, he screwed up his face and groaned. "Euurggh! It tastes of old cheese!"

Milly stuck a finger in the mash and tasted it. "Ugh, he's right."

"You disguised the appearance, but not the taste!" Skribble told Jess, clicking his tiny tongue. "An elementary mistake."

"It's cold, too," complained Jason.

"All right, then," Jess retorted. "*You* be the genie if you think you can do it better!" With that, she flounced back down the spout.

Jason set her free, then whooshed himself inside the lamp. Milly rubbed the sides, and he reemerged in genie form—still with a rude noise but with less of that horrid brown smoke. His green silk suit, funny slippers, and white turban were the same, but this time his moustache was bushier. The curly ends stuck out across his cheeks like huge handlebars.

"A most mystical moustache, boy," said Skribble approvingly. "Milly, make your wish for lunch."

"I've decided I *want* my lunch to be cold," she informed Jason, placing some stale bread on the table. "I want jelly and ice cream, and cake, and triangle sandwiches, and iced buns, and chicken legs. . . ."

Michael rolled his eyes. "We'll be here all day!"

"As you desire!" Jason thundered, and the book vibrated in time with his voice. Suddenly a huge spread of party food appeared.

Michael bit into a chicken leg. "Not bad," he admitted. "Looks and tastes like chicken. . . ."

"But the *texture* is still like stale bread!" Jess pulled a funny face. "If you close your eyes, it's like chicken-flavored stale bread."

"It's still brilliant, Jase," declared Milly. "I'm going to eat a sandwich. That's *meant* to have the texture of bread!" But even she had to admit that the ham in the middle of it seemed very odd.

"My lunch next!" said Michael. "Come on, Milly. Be my genie."

So Milly became the genie and granted Michael's wish for a hamburger that tasted not only of hamburgers but chips and ginger ale as well—a *chamburgle*. She conjured it from a cornflake that Michael found in the bottom of a cereal box left by the bin.

"Not bad," was his verdict. "It's a nice and chewy chamburgle, nothing like a cornflake. And the tastes were all there, mixed up together. Didn't really fill me up, but it saves time eating and drinking everything all in one go!"

"Good," said Jess. "Because I want *my* lunch now!"

Jess described what she wanted to eat—a baked macaroni, tomato, and cheese casserole and a strawberry smoothie. Michael became the genie, whizzing back out of the lamp with an even longer beard than before, and granted her wish.

The casserole looked and smelled delicious—you would never know it had once been some baked beans. The smoothie even came with umbrellas and a slice of pineapple on the rim of the glass.

"Well done, Michael," Jess said grudgingly. "This looks pretty amazing." She stuck a big forkful of casserole into her mouth—and spat it straight out. "Ugh! Rotten eggs!"

"Gotcha!" Michael guffawed and held out his hand for Jason to high-five. Jason looked worriedly at his sister, but since her eyes were closed and watering, he slapped the offered hand just as hard as he could.

"You pig, Michael!" Jess gasped. She took a swig from the smoothie to take away the horrid flavor—but that tasted even worse! "Ugh! It's like cold vomit!"

"This step is all about disguises, isn't it?" Michael asked innocently as Milly quickly fetched Jess a glass of water. "Well, that was just me putting a disguise on top of a disguise!"

"Sly, devious, and underhanded," Skribble piped up from the kitchen counter. "But those are all traits that serve a genie well. . . ."

"Look on the bright side, Jess," said Jason. "We're playing as a team; we should get extra points for that trick!"

"Yes, well, maybe I don't want *him* on my team!" said Jess angrily.

Michael raised his eyebrows. "Why, because I play better than you and make you look like rubbish?"

Jess clenched her fists. "We'll see about that! Genie be free!"

With a yelp of surprise, Michael was sucked down into the spout of the lamp and spat out again on the floor in his normal clothes. Jess grabbed the glass of smoothie and emptied it on his head.

"Urgh!" he cried.

Jumping up, he grabbed the plate of casserole—but before he could throw it over Jess, she yelled, "Genie me!" and vanished back inside the lamp.

"Stop this tomfoolery!" said Skribble, scowling. "This is a serious business!"

Milly grabbed the plate off him, and scraped the casserole into the bin. Jason rubbed the lamp to bring Jess back out as a genie.

"I wish Michael wasn't covered in smoothie," said Jason quickly, "and I wish Jess had a nice taste of strawberries in her mouth."

"It shall be done!" boomed Jess, and she clapped her hands together.

Suddenly, Michael was gunk-free. "Cheers, Jase!" he said with a grin.

"Yeah, thanks, Jason," Jess added, licking her lips. "Truce, Michael?"

"I guess," he said.

"And now I wish there were enough sausages and mash for all of us!" cried Jason.

Jess closed her eyes, then clapped her hands three times. A huge platter of sausage and mash appeared, swimming with rich gravy. And this time, taste and temperature, texture and smell were all spot-on. Too hungry to wish for their own meals all over again, all four children tucked in.

"Would you like some, Skribble?" asked Milly, through a mouthful of sausage.

Skribble shook his head. But he sniffed the air approvingly. "Very good," he said. "You are getting better."

For a while there was silence apart from the sound of chewing and swallowing and forks scraping on the plates.

At last, Michael sat back and gave a satisfied belch. "That was excellent!"

"I suppose we should clean up in here," said Milly. The kitchen was a mess. The bin was overflowing, the washing up lay in a big pile in the sink, and there were boxes and books everywhere.

"If we did, your mum would be well pleased," Michael said. "Hey!" He sat up straight. "We could tidy the whole house—just by disguising its appearance!"

"That's true!" Jason said. "And we could conjure up a really nice dinner for them."

Michael nodded excitedly. "We could say we spent the last pennies of our pitiful allowances on food to make them a surprise dinner." He beamed around. "They needn't know we just used magic and a couple of old baked beans. I bet they'd be so happy, they'd give us some extra cash as a reward. We haven't had a proper allowance since we moved here, and I've got, like, two pennies left now."

"That's tricking them!" said Milly.

"It's not—it's *practice*!" Michael looked at Skribble. "It's doing what the book wants us to do, right, Worm? If it makes us a bit of money on the side, it's not our fault!"

Skribble groaned to himself and disappeared back inside the book.

Jason looked at Jess. "Mum *would* be really happy if the whole house was tidy!"

"Happy enough to splash the cash," Michael agreed.

"Will you shut up about getting money off our parents!" Jess snapped. "You know things are hard for them with the bookshop being about to open."

"Give the money back to them then, if you're so worried," said Michael. "Now, Jase, come on, we're running out of time; they'll be back soon—get wishing!"

Chapter Eleven

The children all took turns to be genie and wish-maker, tidying up the whole house a room at a time. Dust vanished from the dressers and shelves. The washing up put itself in the cupboards. Every last crumb hid itself away, and every last cobweb on the ceiling shriveled to nothing. Soon the whole house was gleaming.

Jess looked around, hands on hips. "This dump is almost livable now!"

"Dad and Ann are going to freak out when they see this!" said Milly happily.

Then they turned their attention to the dinner.

"Nothing too flashy," Jess warned them. "Or Mum and Mark will never believe we did it ourselves."

They went for a simple dinner of egg, potatoes, and peas, with lots of French toast. It was Ann Worthington's favorite. Jess was the one who magicked it into life. They all agreed that her attention to detail was the best—even Michael.

Now they had put the lamp and the book away upstairs, and Milly was watching from the kitchen window for headlights coming up the drive. It was just starting to get dark.

"They're here!" Milly shouted as she saw her dad's car turn into the driveway.

Jess, Jason, Michael, and Milly all bundled out through the kitchen door, wanting to be first to greet their parents.

"Welcome back!" called Jess.

Milly opened the car door and grabbed hold of Ann's arm. "We've got a surprise for you!"

"We've been working really hard all afternoon to tidy the house," said Michael grandly.

"Am I sleeping?" wondered Mark, allowing Jason to help him out of the car. "Have I gone mad?"

"This is just the sort of madness I could get to like!" said Ann. "Michael, could you help me get the shopping bags out of the back of the car?"

"You don't need them, Mum!" said Jess.

"We made you dinner," said Jason, towing her toward the door. "Egg, potatoes, and peas, your favorite!"

"What a lovely thing for you to do." Ann smiled fondly at all of them. "Mark and I have been working so hard all day. I've been up since six, and now it's sunset already. It's really thoughtful of you to help us out like this."

"We just do what little we can," said Michael humbly.

"Come *on*," said Milly, ushering Ann and her dad into the kitchen. "Close your eyes and prepare to be amazed. . . ."

But as they got through the door, it was Milly, Michael, Jess, and Jason who got the biggest shock.

All the steaming hot food had vanished. And the kitchen looked in as bad a state as it always had! Michael made a noise like a small piglet being stepped on.

Mark Worthington opened his eyes and looked around, puzzled. "Food?" he wondered. "Cleaning?"

Ann's face fell a mile. "What's that bread doing on the floor?"

"Um . . . wait till you see the rest of the house!" said Jess quickly, leading them through to the hall. But to her horror, it was the same story here. The shoes lay in a mess, the dust lay thick about, the carpet was muddy. Everything was back just as it had been.

"If this is your idea of a joke, kids, it's not funny." Ann took a deep breath. "I actually thought you might really have been thoughtful for once and . . ."

She trailed off. Jason bit his lip to see tears well up in his mum's eyes. Their plan had gone horribly wrong!

"I don't understand!" said Michael, staring about in dismay.

"Neither do I," said Ann, storming back into the messed-up kitchen and out through the back door. "Looks like I'd better get the *real* dinner on, doesn't it? Frozen pizza!"

She slammed the door behind her.

Mark looked at them. "I think perhaps you all had better clear off for a bit," he said. Then he went outside after Ann.

Michael sighed. He found everyone was looking at him. "What? What did I do?"

"So much for your dumb idea!" said Jess crossly.

"It wasn't just mine; it's . . ." He trailed off. "It's that worm. He messed everything up for us." Michael bunched his fists and charged off upstairs. "This time, I'm *really* gonna squash him!"

"No, Michael!" Milly hissed, running after him. "Don't you dare!"

"Come on," said Jason, grabbing hold of Jess's arm. "We'd better get after them."

They found Michael in Jess and Milly's bedroom, flicking crossly through the pages. "Come out, Worm! Come out and face me like a man!"

"He's not a man; he's a worm!" Milly protested, trying to push Michael away. "Stop it; you'll scare him!"

"I'll splat him!" Michael promised. "Aha!"

"Eek!" squawked Skribble, spluttering out a mouthful of parchment as Michael lunged for him. He ducked down just in time—and Jason and Jess pulled Michael away.

Skribble puffed and pouted crossly. "What is the meaning of this undignified behavior?"

"You mucked up our plan to get in Dad and Ann's good book," said Michael.

"You didn't," said Milly loyally. "Did you, Skribble?"

"I most certainly did not," said Skribble. "Your silly plans came to nothing without my assistance." He looked at them each in turn. "You are trainee genies. And as such, at sunset, any magical act you perform will undo itself."

Jess frowned. "Why?"

"Because otherwise, a trainee may decide that a little magical power is enough for them, and so not to strive to complete the lessons of the great book."

"We have to become real genies for our magic to last," Jason realized.

"Of course you do!" Skribble snapped. "Feeble students that you are, your magic is not strong enough to last beyond the sunset."

Michael shook himself free of Jess's and Jason's grip. "You could've told us!"

"I think I've told you quite enough already," said Skribble. "And you saw fit to pursue your own goals instead of mine—" He had a small but noisy coughing fit. "I mean, instead of the *book's* goals."

"Well, whatever—because of you, we're in trouble now." Michael slumped down on Milly's bed. "Thanks for nothing, Worm."

"We shouldn't have tried to use the book to help ourselves," said Milly quietly. "It sort of serves us right."

Jason sighed. "We should have *really* tidied up. Really cooked Mum and Mark a nice meal. Made an effort."

Suddenly, the book's pages started flicking over and over, this way and that. Skribble squeaked and ducked down.

"What's happening?" said Milly—just as the book stopped on a particular page. "'The Third Step,'" she read out. "'Granting Wishes and Spreading Happiness.'" Her eyes widened. "Hey, it's Step Three! I can read it!"

"That must mean we've passed Step Two!" Jess exclaimed. "Even though we messed up with Mum and Mark."

"The book does not care about your piffling parents," said Skribble. "It is concerned with *you*!"

"Let's see what the judgment is," said Milly excitedly, and the others crowded around her.

At the end of Step Two there was a picture of Jess in her mismatched genie outfit. "That's embarrassing." Jess cringed.

Jason read out the caption: "'From small seeds grow tall flowers.'"

He looked at the next picture. It showed the four of them tidying the house with magic.

"'Appearances can deceive, but a fool is ever a fool. Those who are lazy and seek to profit through magic will ever stumble and fall.'"

"Goody-goody book," muttered Michael.

Jason continued reading, "'HOWEVER! For natural ability, inspired application, and the presence of some good intentions, you have passed this step.'"

"Yes!" cheered Milly. "We won! Even though we all mucked up a bit . . ."

"Perhaps we don't pass each step by doing everything perfectly," said Jason slowly. "Perhaps we get bonus points when we realize we've learned something."

"Of course!" said Jess. "The book doesn't *just* want us to find a lamp and change the appearance of things; it wants us to learn lessons about being genies." She looked at Milly and Michael. "Jase is right. Yesterday the book showed us the next chapter after we'd said that we would be more careful in the future and not rush into stuff. And now we've just agreed we shouldn't wish stuff for ourselves—and so the book has passed us."

Milly turned to Skribble. "Is that true?"

Skribble inclined his head. "It is as they say." He shot them all a look. "And now I am really quite exhausted by you. Come back tomorrow and we shall begin Step Three."

"School starts tomorrow," Jason pointed out. "We won't be able to do any magic until we get home."

"More delays!" Skribble sighed crossly.

"Sorry," Jess said. "But we really can't miss school, however much we'd *like* to." Everyone in her new class already had friends to hang around with and she had no one. She wasn't looking forward to going back at all.

"We'll come and find you as soon as we get home," Milly promised.

"Very well," Skribble said shortly. "Tomorrow, then. Good evening."

"Bye, Skribble!" Milly called. But he had already dived back into the book. She closed it up and slid it beneath her pillow. "I hope he's not too cross with us."

"Never mind the worm, never mind Dad and Ann—we passed!" Michael grinned. "We rock! Our magic was good—it's not our fault sunset came along when it did."

"But I'm really hungry now," said Jason. "It's like we haven't had any lunch at all."

"I guess we haven't," said Jess.

"Let's see what's *really* for tea," said Milly. "It may not be as lovely as the stuff we came up with, but I don't care. I just want Dad and Ann to like us again."

They went downstairs. There was a lot of banging and slamming going on in the kitchen. With nervous looks, they all filed inside. Mark and Ann were unpacking the shopping bags in frosty silence.

Michael cleared his throat. "Sorry about that," he said. "We, uh . . . we dreamed we'd done all the tidying up—"

"Oh, don't bother," said Ann wearily.

"We've decided that we should *all* tidy up the house," said Mark. "Tonight. And then you can get your things ready for school."

Michael groaned, but Jess elbowed him. "It's not like we can get on with anything else, is it?" she murmured.

"But first, we'll have tea," said Ann, holding up a thin, beige box.

"Frozen pizza," said Milly.

Jess put on a weak smile. "I like frozen pizza!"

Well, I don't *like it here,* thought Michael. Living in Moreways Meet was getting them all down. *Once we're genies, we'll go straight back to London. Dad with a proper job, me with a regular allowance, no Jess to boss me about . . .*

He sighed as the ancient oven buzzed and rattled into life. *And no more frozen pizza—ever!*

At eight o'clock the next morning, the kitchen was a whirl of activity.

"Jason! Milly! Here are your lunch boxes," said Ann, handing them out. She went to the stairs and shouted, "Michael! You're going to be late!"

Jason tugged on his sneakers. "Where are my gym shorts, Mum?"

"Here." Ann grabbed them from the sideboard. "And here are yours, Milly. Get your coats on and I'll walk you to school."

"Where's my backpack?" wailed Milly, looking through the kitchen cupboards and drawers.

"Try the laundry room," said Ann, running a hand through her hair. She caught sight of Jess gloomily eating a piece of toast at the kitchen table. "You okay, Jess?"

"Yeah," Jess muttered. But she wasn't. She was dreading the thought of school. It had been bad enough when she had started just before Easter, but at least then she'd known she only had to suffer through two weeks before the holidays. Now the whole term was stretching out in front of her. A term with no friends, no one to sit with in lessons, no one to hang around with at break time. *I wish we were still in London,* she thought unhappily, for about the millionth time.

Her mum hurried to the stairs again. "Michael! Come on!"

Milly started throwing shoes out of the cupboard in the laundry room. "I can't find my backpack!" she exclaimed. "It's gone! It's really gone!"

"No, it isn't; it's here." Jess picked it up off the table and thrust it at Milly. "I'm going," she announced, grabbing her coat and crossing to the door.

"Aren't you going to wait for Michael?" Ann asked.

"No," Jess said firmly. There was no way she was going to walk to school with her younger stepbrother and all his new mates. How sad would that look?

"Milly, please can you put all those shoes back. Jason, you need your other coat. . . ." Ann looked wearily at Jess. "And I hope you all have a good day!"

"Yeah, right," Jess muttered under her breath as she let the door slam behind her. "Like that's ever going to happen."

It was as bad as Jess had feared. She'd had a faint hope that there might be some other new people starting that term, but no, it was still just her—the new girl on her own. At lunchtime, she sat by herself eating her packed lunch.

She took a book to read so she could pretend she wanted to sit on her own, but she knew deep down it wouldn't fool anyone.

Jess's heart sank as a gang of girls from her class came to sit at the table next to her. She tried not to watch them but her eyes kept straying over the top of her book. Colette Jones, the most popular girl in Jess's class, sat at one end of the table and all the other girls arranged themselves around her. *Colette and the Colette Clones,* Jess thought sourly, noticing how three of the other girls in the group had their hair tied back in exactly the same type of pony-tail as their leader. They were even wearing the same shade of lip gloss. Colette began to talk about a trip to London during the holidays.

Jess tried not to listen but Colette's clear voice kept carrying across to her.

"There was this amazing green top that I bought . . . and at Harrods I bought some blush and this eyeliner . . . then we went to this coffee bar . . . oh, and I saw Gwyneth Paltrow there! It was so cool. . . ." Colette waved her hands around expressively as her friends *oo*ed and *ah*ed.

Oh, puh-lease, Jess thought to herself, trying to pretend she wasn't interested. There were other things in life apart from clothes, makeup, and celebrities. "I've got a magic genie handbook at home," she muttered, trying to console herself. "If you knew that then you'd really have something to talk about. . . ."

"I can't believe you saw Gwyneth Paltrow!" said one of Colette's friends. "That's so, like . . . wow!"

Jess rolled her eyes but unfortunately, just at that moment, Colette glanced across at her. Jess hastily tried to change her eye roll into a thoughtful frown, as if there was something *very* interesting in her book. She put her lunch away and got hastily to her feet. She might not want to be friends with Colette and her clones, but she certainly didn't want to be their enemy either.

As she stood up, Colette cast another look in her direction. She was frowning. Jess looked away, and Colette said something that she didn't catch. Someone else replied in a low voice and everyone laughed. Jess blushed. She was sure they were talking about her. She hurried out of the lunch hall, her cheeks burning. *I hate this school,* she thought bitterly. *I hate living in Moreways Meet!* She thought again of *The Genie Handbook*, and of what they would have to do next to get out of here. . . .

When Jess got home after school, Michael was leaning on the gateway, surrounded by a group of boys, talking and laughing.

Jess sighed and went into the house, shutting the door

with a bang. It wasn't fair. Her stupid stepbrother had made friends so easily. She walked into the kitchen and dumped her bag on the floor.

Jason was sitting at the table, eating a packet of crisps. "Hi, Jess. You okay?"

"Ecstatic," Jess sighed. "Where's everyone else?"

"Mum and Mark are at the shop and Milly's upstairs in your bedroom."

"Oh, great. Making more mess, I imagine," Jess muttered.

Jason looked at his sister in surprise. "What's up with you?"

Jess shrugged. "Just school. It's rubbish still." She took a crisp from him and crunched it gloomily. "How are you getting on?"

"Okay," Jason replied. "We got to go on the computers loads today, and me, Matthew, and Ryan finished the worksheet ages before anyone else. . . ."

"Yay you," muttered Jess.

Just then the kitchen door opened and Milly came in with *The Genie Handbook*. "Jess, you're back! Fab. When can we start Step Three?"

"Just as soon as *your* brother gets his butt in here," Jess replied grumpily.

"I'll go and get him," Milly offered. Pulling on her

sneakers, she ran out of the house. Jess and Jason watched as she barged into the group and spoke to Michael. Michael looked irritated for a moment but then shrugged, said good-bye, and let Milly drag him inside.

"So you've finally decided to stop talking to your friends, have you?" Jess remarked bitterly.

"Least I've *got* friends. Not like you, Miss Billie no-mates!" Jess glared, but Michael didn't even notice as he headed for the den. "Come on, then. It's magic time!"

They hurried down the stairs. Michael threw himself on the sofa and Milly and Jason crouched on the floor with the book. Jess stood tensely by the door, her arms folded. *I really hate Michael,* she thought. *I want to go back to London.* To her horror she felt tears prickle at the backs of her eyes. She blinked them away furiously before joining the others.

"Let's see what we have to do next," said Jason. "Shall I read it out?" They all nodded. Jason cleared his throat and leaned forward. . . .

The Genie Handbook

The Third Step:
Granting Wishes and
Spreading Happiness

YOU WHO ARE WITNESS
TO THESE WORDS!

By now, you are on your way to granting wishes with polish and precision. But you must gain a full understanding of the old maxim: "Beware of what you wish for—it may come true." A wise genie will always perceive perils as well as welcoming rewards. UNDERSTAND THIS WELL! To have a wish come true is akin to finding a shortcut as you wander along the winding path of fate. But the direction in which it leads you may be false.

NOW! You may hear many wishes, and truly you should grant them as you continue along the path of genie training. But REMEMBER—magic can be a maze, and the way is seldom clear—so think hard, perceive danger, and keep tight hold on that which is precious to you.

Chapter Twelve

"What does all *that* mean?" Milly said, confused.

"I'm not sure." Jason read the words again. "'You may hear many wishes. . . .'"

Milly smiled. "Maybe it means we're allowed to hear each other's wishes and make them come true!"

"Hey, Worm!" Michael called. "What do you think?"

Scribble's head popped up from the book. "I think that you are a rude and impertinent boy! Now, hurry up and grant each other's wishes, you deplorable dunces!"

Jess felt a thrill of excitement. "You really think that's what it wants?"

"Of course I do!" said Skribble. "Who's going first? You have the perfect opportunity to impress the book with your developing powers!"

"I'll be the genie first!" said Milly. "Genie me!"

She whizzed into the lamp.

"You!" Skribble was peering at Jason. "You, younger boy! Make a wish!"

Jason picked up the lamp and rubbed it, remembering his list. Milly the genie shot out in a drift of silver smoke. "What is your wish?"

"I . . . I wish there was world peace!"

Michael looked disgusted. "That is so lame!"

"And utterly impossible," Skribble snapped. "Peace only comes to a human when he has attained his heart's desire, and even then not for long. . . ." He shook his head. "Foolish boy, not even the greatest genie can satisfy a hundred billion wishes at once!"

"Phew," said Milly.

"That is why a genie only appears to one person at a time," Skribble went on. "To whomever rubs the lamp."

"Anyway, whatever we wish for, it's only till sunset," Michael pointed out. "What good is one afternoon of world peace, you muppet?"

Jason blushed. "Um . . . in that case . . . I wish I had a never-ending supply of chocolate!"

"Your wish is my command!" Milly boomed.

There was a flash of silver light and Jason felt the pockets of his jeans get suddenly heavy. He shoved his hands in and pulled out a chocolate bar from each pocket. "Cool!" He looked at the bars—one was filled with caramel and one with raisins and nuts. "Hey, they're even different types."

"Course!" Milly said smugly. "It'd be boring just to eat the same kind of chocolate all the time." She did a twirl. "Just call me superawesome magnificent Milly the genie!"

Jason ripped the paper from one of the chocolate bars and stuffed as much chocolate as he could into his mouth. "They taste good, too!" He reached for his pockets. "And every time I take one out, another one appears!"

"Good wish, mate," Michael said approvingly as he helped himself to a bar. "Go on, get back in the lamp, Milly. It's my turn now!"

Once Milly was back in the lamp, Jason said the spell of release: "Genie be free," said Jason.

Milly shot out with a whoop of exhilaration. Then she wished herself back into the lamp: "Genie me!" she shouted.

No sooner was she inside than Michael was rubbing the old brass sides. "I wish for the power to look through stuff—like Superman's X-ray vision!"

Milly whooshed out, just as before. "Your wish is my command," she boomed, clapping her hands. She grinned at them all. "Hey, this is fun!"

Michael blinked.

"Did it work?" asked Jason, excited.

"Whoa!" Michael stared around the room. "You lot look really weird. I can see through your top layer of clothes! Nice Batman underpants, Jase!"

"Michael!" Jess exclaimed. As he looked over at her she grabbed a throw from the sofa and wrapped it around herself. "Don't you dare look at me! Stop it!"

"It's my turn now!" said Milly. "I know exactly what I'm going to wish for. Free me, Michael, and then you have a go at being the genie." Her voice grew fainter as she jumped back into the lamp.

"Genie be free!" said Michael. "And genie *me*!" He whooshed into the lamp just as Milly whooshed back out.

"I wish for a pony!" said Milly breathlessly, rubbing away at the lamp.

Now Michael shot out of the lamp in his black ninja genie outfit and enormous beard, and clapped his hands. "It shall be done!" The next second, a small, fat brown pony with a shaggy mane and tail and blue head collar was standing in the basement. It had a very surprised expression on its face.

"It's real!" Jess gasped.

Milly dropped the lamp and hugged the pony. Then she looked accusingly at Michael. "It's cute, but it's not very big."

"You just said you wanted a pony," Michael protested. "You didn't say what size."

The pony snorted.

"You're the genie! You should think about the details!" Milly told Michael. "You should have known I'd want one I could ride." She stroked the pony quickly, hoping its feelings wouldn't be hurt. "Well, you're still nice. What am I going to call you, boy?"

"What about 'Dogfood'?" Michael suggested.

"Don't be horrible!" Milly cried. "I'll call him . . . Toffee!"

"*Gloopy*, more like," said Michael, pulling a face. "I can see through its skin! I can see all the blood going around and stuff." His face turned pale. "Oh, that is *so* gross. UGH!" He quickly disappeared back into the lamp.

Jess grabbed the lamp from the floor. "It's my turn now."

"Well, I wish that Jess could have my next wish," said Milly, patting Toffee.

Michael whooshed back out, still looking a bit green. "What is your wish?" he cried, and the book trembled.

Jess felt a tremble go through her as well. *Keep tight hold on that which is precious to you,* the book had told them. *Well, I know what's precious to me,* she thought. *And I'm never going to let go.*

Her heart pounded. It was the moment she'd been waiting for. "I wish . . . I wish we were all back in London!"

"What?" Milly gasped.

"No, Jess!" Michael spluttered, but his hands were already clapping themselves together and his voice was booming out: "Your wish is my command!"

Milly saw Jason grab the book. There was a bright red flash. Milly screamed as the world went instantly dark and began to spin. There was the sound of something metal being dropped and a pony's worried whinny. Milly felt herself tumbling over and over and over. . . .

And then suddenly she landed on her feet. At the same moment the lights seemed to come back on.

Milly blinked. The first thing she saw was Jess's, Michael's, and Jason's shocked faces. Then she saw Toffee, snorting with alarm. There was the sound of cars and hooting horns close by. Suddenly Milly realized they weren't inside the house anymore. There was a gray sky above them and the faded rug in the basement had gone. They were standing on concrete. With a sinking feeling, she looked around. They were in the middle of a parking lot beside a main road. The traffic was bumper-to-bumper, and horns were blaring.

Milly's eyes widened. "We really *are* in London!"

"But whereabouts?" said Jess. She turned toward Michael. "I wanted us to be back where we used to live."

Michael groaned. "You could have said. Details, remember?"

"You're the genie!" Jess retorted. "You're the one who's supposed to think about the details!"

"Yeah, right! Blame it on me!" Michael hid his face in his beard. "You should have said where you wanted to go!"

"Get us out of here, Jess!" Jason urged as chocolate bars began to overflow from his pockets. "Make another wish." He saw some passersby looking at them curiously. "Quickly!"

"Okay," Jess sighed. She looked around. "Where's the lamp?"

They all stared at each other.

"You were holding it, Jess, when you made the wish," said Jason. "What did you do with it?"

Jess's face paled. "I . . . think I might have dropped it back in the den."

There was a silence, broken only by the thud of falling chocolate bars.

"No," Michael said, shaking his head. "You're not going to tell me we haven't got the lamp?"

Jess felt her cheeks burn red. She gave a small nod.

"Perfect!" Michael looked at her furiously. "What was it the book said—'keep tight hold on that which is precious'? What's more precious than the lamp? You heard the worm: Without a lamp a genie is nothing!"

"Michael can't grant any wishes, otherwise," cried Milly. "None of us can!" The wall of traffic rumbled beside them. "We're stuck here!"

"Everyone stay calm," ordered Jess. "The magic will wear off at sunset; that's only a couple of hours away. . . ."

"A couple of hours?" said Michael. He looked particularly strange standing in his black genie outfit with curly-toed slippers in the middle of a parking lot. "I can't stick this for a couple of hours! My X-ray vision is getting stronger. I can see through *everything*!" He shut his eyes and groaned. "I can even see through my eyelids! It's making me feel really sick. What about the book? Do you have the book?"

"Yes," said Jason. He turned to the right pages. "But it's still all gibberish. Skribble?" He shook the book a bit, and winced as two large chocolate bars fell onto his foot. "Skribble, please!"

"I'm busy," came a grumbly voice. "Bother me when you've finished making your wishes."

"But we *have* finished!" cried Jason.

"Or rather, we *are* finished." Michael glared at Jess, snatched the book, and shoved it into a large side pocket of his black jacket. "I bet that stupid worm wouldn't know how to help us anyway. And I certainly don't want to see through *his* revolting body!"

A battered blue van rumbled into the parking lot. Toffee neighed in alarm. Milly hung on tight to his lead rope. "Whoa! Steady, boy." He tugged her forward. "Hey, guys! Any chance of some help here? He's small but he's really strong."

Jason went over to her, chocolate spilling from his pockets with every step. The pony squealed and kicked out at him. "Hey, stop it!" Jason cried, slipping on a fruit-and-nut bar as he tried to get out of the way.

Toffee bit Milly's arm and she yelled.

"What are we going to do?" Michael exclaimed. He looked at Jess and stared. "Oh . . . my . . . !"

"You'd better not be looking at my underwear!" she told him furiously.

"Not your underwear." Michael's face turned a shade of green. "The X-ray vision's getting worse. I can see your skeleton! All the bones and bits of gristle and your *brain*! Ugh . . ." He turned, staggered behind a car, and was sick—very, very noisily.

"Oh, nice!" said Jess, revolted.

"Help!" Milly wailed as Toffee yanked the lead rope out of her hands and careered off toward the parking lot exit. "Quick! We've got to stop him! If he gets out into the road, he might get hurt!"

"He's not the only one!" Jason yelled.

119

They all charged after the pony, Michael groaning and clutching his stomach.

As Jess ran, she felt her eyes filling with tears. She'd set her heart on coming back to London, but not like this. *Never* like this!

Chapter Thirteen

Toffee cantered out of the parking lot and down the street. Astonished passersby leaped out of his way.

"Come back, Toffee!" Milly wailed, charging after him. "Please!"

A mother tutted. "What are a bunch of kids doing out on their own with a horse?"

"Where are your parents?" shouted an old man.

Ignoring him, Milly forced herself to run faster. If she could only reach Toffee and grab hold of his lead rope . . .

"I can see through the pavement," groaned Michael behind her. "I can see the sewers. I can see rats in the sewers! I can see what the rats have been *eating* in the sewers. Urrrgh . . ."

Toffee met a crowd of people walking along the pavement. Slowing down, he flattened his ears and lunged for a businessman's arm. The man staggered back with a cry and fell into a workmen's tent with a noisy clatter.

"Call the police!" someone roared.

"Got you!" cried Milly triumphantly, grabbing hold of Toffee's lead rope, but the pony was too alarmed by the shouts of pedestrians and the honking of horns to hold still. He set off down a side street, with Milly hanging on.

Jess rushed after her and grabbed the lead rope too, but Toffee was too strong to be stopped.

"Help us!" Jess yelled as Toffee towed her and Milly out of the side street, toward the main road.

Michael had stopped to be sick down a drain, but Jason managed to lend his strength to the pony's lead rope. With three of them pulling, Toffee came to a stop.

"We've got to get away from here," said Jess. "To the park."

"There's a crosswalk over there!" Jason pointed, and a Nestlé Crunch bar fell out of his sleeve. "Come on!"

Between the three of them they pulled and coaxed Toffee farther up the street while Michael followed weakly behind. Drivers in cars stared. A motorbike courier veered off the road and crashed into a concrete pole.

"We're going to cause a real pileup!" Jason fretted. On the other side of the road there was a line of tall trees. "If we could only find cover . . ."

"Seems to me Toffee had the right idea," Michael muttered. "Let's go with his first plan—just *run*!" So saying, he grabbed a handful of Toffee's tail, shut his eyes tight, and thwacked his hand against the horse's backside.

Toffee tore free of Jess, Milly, and Jason and plunged across the road toward the trees, dragging Michael along behind. "Who needs a guide dog!" Michael yelled, clutching tightly to the pony's tail. Cars skidded to a halt on either side of the crossing, blaring their horns.

"Michael, you lunatic!" Jess yelled.

Then the pony pushed through the tall trees, and with a yelp Michael crashed through after him.

Jason led the way over the crossing in pursuit. They battled through the trees and emerged in a large park. Luckily, there weren't many people about, and those who looked over ignored them. Toffee was standing in the shade of a willow tree, calmer now that he was away from the traffic, and Michael was slumped against the tree trunk.

Jess marched over. "That was so dumb, Michael. You and Toffee could have been hurt!"

"I could see through those trees," he told her. "I knew there was a park on the other side. Maybe I *could* have been hurt—but I didn't want to risk anyone else getting injured on the road because they were staring at us!"

"Oh," said Jess. She had to admit the explanation sounded pretty sensible. But she was still feeling cross, so she didn't say so. Instead she kicked at the pile of Milky Ways growing up around Jason's feet. Toffee nosed one aside as he began to graze, flicking his tail.

"I want to go home," said Jason quietly. "Back to Moreways Meet."

"That stupid house isn't a home; it's just the place we all live." Michael sighed. "Even so, I wish we were back there too—"

"Shush." Milly waved her hands, suddenly concentrating. "I can hear . . ."

"Sirens," Jess concluded. She could hear the electronic wail now too.

They all looked at each other in alarm.

"Let's hide!" said Jason.

But Michael shook his head. "No point. The cops will just follow the trail of chocolate, sick, and horse poo."

"Toffee hasn't pooed," said Milly defensively.

Michael eyed the pony's backside grimly. "You can't see what's coming."

"There's still an hour and a half till it gets dark." Jason fretted. "You're right, Michael, the police *will* find us, and they'll take our names and address and even if we vanish at sunset they'll drive over to our house and Mum'll find out and—"

"Skribble!" Milly exclaimed. She bent and pulled *The Genie Handbook* from Michael's pocket. "Skribble will help us; I *know* he will. Where is he?"

"He's probably stuffing his face," Michael muttered. "Or else he's asleep."

"Asleep?" came a familiar, muffled cry. "Asleep, with all the commotion you have been causing, you churlish chitterlings?"

"Please, Skribble," Milly implored the bookworm. "Please, kind, wonderful Skribble, can you help us?"

Skribble tutted. "I deduce that you have no lamp, my dear Milly. And so, I'm afraid, there is little you can do."

The sirens were getting very loud now. "But if we wait here till sunset we'll be caught," said Jason.

"And they'll throw us into prison and lock us up for ages," said Michael.

"Locked up again?" The worm trembled. "No!"

"What do you mean?" Jess frowned. "Locked up . . . *again?*"

Skribble stared at her, apparently dumbfounded for a moment. "Er, nothing. Simply a figure of speech . . . about being stuck in here." He looked sharply at each of the children. "Now, before I agree to help, do you promise to try harder with your training?"

Jess and Jason nodded. Michael gave a grunt.

"Very well," said Skribble as the sirens rose in pitch and volume. "You must find a metal container. With a little magical assistance, the container can be used as a temporary lamp—good for one wish only."

"Like a sort of emergency exit!" Jason realized.

Jess stared around. "But where are we going to find a metal container?"

"Would an empty soda can be all right?" asked Milly.

Michael squinted at a nearby bin. "There're a couple in there. Look out for the wasp in the one nearest the top."

Jason forced a path out through his minor mountain of chocolate bars. Just as he reached the bin, the shriek of the sirens suddenly stopped.

"Quick!" Michael hissed, staring at the trees, frowning, and blinking as he used his X-ray vision. "The police have parked on the road over there. They'll find us dead easy. We've got two minutes, tops, to get out of this!"

Chapter Fourteen

Jason rummaged around in the bin. "I've found one of those cans," he cried, pulling it out. "It's a bit squashed—"

"It'll do," said Jess, snatching it from him. "Now, what must we do, Skribble?"

The bookworm puffed himself up grandly. "I must recite an incantation. Set down the container. Older boy, you stand beside it."

"The police!" Jess croaked. Two officers were pushing their way through the line of trees.

Skribble quickly cleared his throat and began to recite:

"Meg-deb, mug-dub, mig-dib, dun—
Grant us one wish, O base metal, just one.
Dub-mig, deb-mug, dib-meg, doo—
A lamp be thy guise and thy magic be true!"

With a flash and a cloud of cabbage-scented smoke,

Michael was sucked up inside the can.

"Hey, you kids!" called one of the officers.

"They're *coming*!" hissed Milly.

"Argh!" came Michael's faint cry from inside the can. "There's a wasp in here!"

"Sorry!" Jason wailed.

"Don't sting him," Jess muttered, rubbing the can. "Don't sting him *yet*, anyway. . . ."

Michael the genie swirled out of the can.

"Quickly, girl!" commanded Skribble. "And get it right! Remember, you only have one chance—one single wish. . . ."

The nearest policeman was just a few strides away now. "We've had complaints that you kids and your horse have been running wild. . . ."

Jess closed her eyes and reeled off the wish: "I wish that Jason, Milly, Michael, and I were back in the den in our house in Moreways Meet just after sunset!"

"Wishing won't get you out of this," said the officer gravely.

"You'd better be wrong," muttered Michael. And he clapped his hands.

The world started to spin, just as it had done before. Jess felt the ground melt away beneath her feet and for a long moment she felt like she was floating. Then there was a bump and she knew she was standing on something solid again.

She staggered forward, barely daring to open her eyes. Then relief flooded through her as she saw the sofa, the bean-bags, the ancient stereo on a packing case. And she was still clutching the crumpled can in both hands. A wasp wafted out of it and flew smack into the small window before collapsing to the dusty sill beneath. Outside it was dusk.

"We're back!" Jason yelled. He checked his pockets, disbelievingly. "And no chocolate!"

"No Toffee either," Milly realized, staring all around, still holding on tight to the handbook. "Where's he gone?"

"It's after sunset," said Jess, still stunned. "Just what I wished for."

"Then . . . he disappeared as the magic wore off," said Milly forlornly. "I never even said good-bye."

"Hang on, where's Michael?" said Jason, frowning. "If it's after sunset and we can't do any more magic—"

"OOOF!" In another thick cloud of smoke, Michael was spat out of the can, back in his normal clothes.

"Hey," Jess told him with a smile. "You did it. You got us home!"

"Huh?" He stared around in amazement. "Wow . . . I really *did* do it, didn't I! And—" He blinked. "My eyes are back to normal!"

Jess sat down heavily on the squashy sofa. "I'm glad that's over. Today has *not* been fun."

"Next time we've got to think really carefully about what we wish for," said Jason. "We could have gotten into so much trouble!"

Milly nodded with feeling. "Wishes can go wrong so easily."

Michael rubbed his aching stomach. "And we must never, *ever* forget the lamp again." He clapped Jason on the back. "If you hadn't picked up the book, Jase—"

Just then, Skribble poked his head out. "Is everyone back safely?" he asked, and Milly was sure there was worry in his little eyes.

"Yes, we are," said Milly in relief. "Thank you for helping us, Skribble."

"We made a real mess of things," said Jason. He thought about the chaos they had caused. "What will all those people in London be thinking?"

"They won't be thinking anything, will they?" said Milly. "It's after sunset, so everything will be back to normal."

"Not quite," said Skribble.

The children stared at him. "What do you mean?" said

Jess. "You told us yesterday that our magic wore off at sunset."

"Perhaps I did," said Skribble. "But as you progress through the steps of training, your magic becomes stronger. Of course, until you become full genies, your magical creations will vanish at sunset and people's memories of them will cloud and fade. But in the meantime, now you have completed Step Three. . . ." He swung around to Milly. "Does your arm still hurt where Toffee bit it, my child?"

"Yes," Milly realized, rubbing her arm. "Yes, it does."

Skribble nodded gravely. "You see? Unless a wish-maker wishes it, the physical *effects* of the magic will remain."

"So, that motorcycle *will* have crashed into the pole today?" said Jess.

Milly looked worried. "And that businessman will have been bitten too?"

"Yes. As you say in your modern way of speaking, you *have* indeed made a 'real mess of things.'" Skribble sniffed. "The book is not pleased with your progress. Not pleased at all."

He ducked down inside the book, and the pages fluttered over to the end of Step Three. New pictures had appeared.

"There we are in the parking lot," said Jason.

Jess cringed to see herself looking so flustered and afraid.

The book's comment didn't make her feel any better:

Badly prepared, ill-thought-out wishes, granted lazily.

"Oh, come on, I wasn't lazy!" Michael argued. "If I'd been lazy, I would have zapped us a mile down the road or something."

The next picture showed Jess looking very guilty and Michael looking furious.

Without a worthy vessel, a genie is unworthy, was the book's only comment.

"I should never have dropped the lamp," said Jess, feeling tired and miserable.

"We wouldn't have passed this step anyway," said Jason, staring at a picture of them running after Toffee, spilling chocolate everywhere and scaring passersby. The caption underneath read:

Thoughtless exposure of magic in the commonplace invites needless danger and questions that must not be answered.

Milly sighed. "What does that even mean?"

"I think it means that we should never have gone out on a busy road when we had so much magic going on," Jason told her. "We must have scared loads of people, as well as nearly causing a lot of crashes."

The last picture was of Michael charging across the road with a handful of horse tail.

Courage and consideration for others around are valuable qualities, the book stated.

"Well, that sounds a bit better," said Michael. "But there's no getting away from it; we messed up big-time." He straightened and sighed. "I still feel funny after that X-ray vision. I'm going to lie down."

"We can try to pass the step again tomorrow," Jason said optimistically.

The others nodded slowly.

They left the den, feeling very subdued. At the top of the stairs, they all went their different ways—Jason and Michael to their rooms, Jess and Milly to their bedroom to hide the book.

As she shut the door behind them, Milly carefully opened the book again and checked the page where Step Four should have begun.

There was nothing to see but squiggles in the dark, mysterious ink.

Chapter Fifteen

That night, Milly couldn't sleep. She wasn't just thinking about *The Genie Handbook*, but about her dad and Ann as well. When they'd lived in London in separate houses, they had hardly ever argued. But now it was all they ever did. Just like at supper this evening. Ann had been cross because her dad had signed up for some big town trivia contest that Saturday—just a day before the bookshop opened.

Milly sighed. She didn't like it when they argued. *Maybe we can use magic to help them,* she thought. She felt her pillowcase. The book lay inside it, silent and still. It was hard to believe there was anything magic about it at all.

But there was. The memories of being in London that day were still vivid in her mind. She blushed as she remembered the shocked looks on people's faces as Toffee towed her down the street. She wondered what had happened to him. Where would he have gone?

"Skribble," she whispered to the pillowcase. "Are you awake?"

There was a quiet rustling; then Skribble's voice carried through the pillow. "What is it, Milly?"

"I . . ." She hesitated, then sighed. "I was just thinking about Toffee. What happened to him after we left? Is he okay?"

"Do not worry, Milly," said Skribble. "He was a pony made by magic, and so back to magic he went. There is nothing to be concerned about."

Milly felt better. Even though Toffee had been very bad-tempered, she hated to think of him lost somewhere. "I'm sorry we failed Step Three, Skribble," she whispered. "If we get another chance, we'll try harder, I promise. We'll think about what dangers the wishes will put us in and try to make sure we never let other people see anything magic happening from now on. It was really stupid of us." She yawned. "Thank you for telling me that Toffee's all right, though. You're a lovely worm. I don't care if we never become genies; I'm going to look after you forever and ever."

Skribble did not reply. *He must have gone to sleep,* Milly thought. And a few moments later, she had gone to sleep too.

She was in the middle of a dream about a magic riding hat that kept shaking on her head when she woke with a start, blinked, and then realized that her head really *was* shaking. She gasped and sat up in alarm. Then she realized that it wasn't her head; it was her pillow.

The book!

Milly pulled out the book. Rainbow flashes of light glimmered over its cover, lighting up the dark of the bedroom. As it fell onto the bed the cover flew open and the pages started flipping over.

Milly jumped off the bed. "Jess!" she hissed, shaking her stepsister awake.

"What is it? What's going on?" Jess said in confusion.

"The book! Something's happening! It's doing what it usually does when we've passed a step." As Milly spoke, the pages stopped turning and the sparks flickered and went out.

Turning her bedside light on, Jess got out of bed. She went over to the book. Two sentences stood out at the end of Step Three, the words clear and dark:

Courage, compassion, and care serve a genie well. You have passed Step Three.

"We've passed!" Jess gasped in surprise. "But how? We made such a mess of everything!"

"You passed by the skin of your teeth and the tips of your toenails," said a tetchy voice. Skribble poked his head out of a hole in the book's cover. "You were, as the scholars say, a borderline pass or fail. The book has been evaluating your performance and your reactions and has decided that you deserve to pass. Goodness knows why. One question about a pony and a few regrets—soppy, sentimental, ridiculous book!" He tutted and looked away, but Milly was sure she caught sight of a smile on his little face.

"I can't believe we've passed!" she exclaimed. "Let's tell the boys!"

"Not now," Jess said quickly, shushing her. "We might wake up Mum and Mark. Let's wait until the morning. It can be our secret till then."

Milly smiled. "Okay."

"First thing in the morning, mind," said Skribble, yawning. "There is still much to be done. And as you have all agreed, you must work a good deal harder."

"Good night, lovely Skribble," Milly said, picking up the book. "We'll see you then."

"Good night, Milly," the bookworm replied sleepily.

Milly closed the book and tucked it carefully under her pillow and settled down. *Step Four!* That meant there were just three more steps to pass and then they got to be proper genies. *Then we'll be able to have wishes that don't stop at sunset,* she thought. She sighed happily and shut her eyes.

On the other side of the room, Jess lay awake. There was only one wish burning in *her* mind. To go back to London. *Not like we did today,* she decided. *But properly. To go back to our old lives, before Mum and Mark were married, and* stay *there.*

She hesitated. To be separate families again instead of one big one—was that what she really wanted?

Of course it is, she thought firmly.

"Time to get up, girls!" Ann Worthington banged on the door in the morning. "You're going to be late."

Milly sat up and checked the alarm clock. Quarter to eight. She groaned and jumped out of bed. She'd meant to be up early to have a chance to talk to Jason and Michael. "Come on, Jess, we've got to tell the boys about the book!"

"Later." Jess groaned and buried her face in the pillow.

Milly pulled on her robe and ran to Jason's room, but he'd already gone downstairs. She raced up to Michael's room instead and banged on the door. "It's me, Michael! You'll never guess what; the book says—"

"It's too early, Milly!" Michael groaned.

"But . . ."

"Go away!" he snapped.

Milly stamped her foot in frustration and then headed back downstairs. Jason would be excited by her news. She knew he would. But when she got to the kitchen she found Jason deep in conversation with her dad.

"What type of animal is a natterjack?" Jason was asking.

"A toad?" Milly's dad replied.

"Good," said Jason. "Tell me what the next three prime numbers in this sequence are: 1, 3, 5, 7, 11 . . ."

"Um . . ." Mark Worthington looked worried. "Now let me think. . . ."

"What are you doing?" Milly asked curiously.

"Practicing," her dad answered. "For the Trivia Team Challenge at the town hall on Saturday." He shook his head. "Will you help me again tonight, Jason? Maybe you could think up some more questions for me after school."

"Sure." Jason looked pleased.

Milly suddenly remembered what she had come into the kitchen for. She pulled Jason's arm. "I read something in a book last night I wanted to tell you about."

Jason's eyes widened. Milly dragged him out of the kitchen.

"So what is it?" he said as they hurried up the stairs.

"We've passed!" Milly hissed.

"What?" Jason's whole face lit up. "Let's see!"

They went into the bedroom. Jess was now dressed and brushing her hair. "I'm trying to get ready for school. Go away, Jason!"

"He can't," said Milly. "He's come to see the book!"

The door opened behind her and Michael shambled in. "So, what's going on, Mil?"

"Argh! It's like Piccadilly Circus around here!" Jess moaned.

"We wish," said Michael. "At least it would be closer to home."

"Aha!" Milly's eyes were gleaming with her news. "But we're now a step nearer to getting there!"

Milly opened the book with a flourish. "Ta-da!"

For a fleeting moment, she had a horrible thought. What if she'd dreamed everything the night before? But no—there were the words at the end of Step Three saying that they had passed, and there was Step Four, clear and ready for them to read.

The Genie Handbook

The Fourth Step:
Identifying a Worthy Wish-Maker

YOU WHO ARE WITNESS
TO THESE WORDS!

You are now well aware of the importance of crafting a wish with precision and foreseeing the dangers that might arise. In the last step you indulged each other's frivolous fancies and foolish fripperies. But now the time has come to grant wishes for other wish-makers. Any attempt to grant your own or each other's wishes in this stage will lead to INSTANT DISQUALIFICATION.

NEVER FORGET! The heart's desire of a deserving soul is as precious as the first birdsong of spring, and a genie must treat it as tenderly as a newborn babe.

For this, the fourth step of your training, you must identify a soul deserving of magical enrichment—someone whose life could be transformed by the granting of a single, heartfelt wish. And, once this person is precisely pinpointed, you must *contrive to cure his ills through the granting of a great MAGICK—at least until sunset. . . .*

FEAR NOT! Should the step be successfully completed, his mind will be washed clean of the boon bestowed upon him. And yet, in spite of this, he will surely come to know happiness.

Chapter Sixteen

"Wow," breathed Milly as she finished reading. "So, we'll be doing magic for someone else . . . like proper genies!"

Jason nodded nervously. "What if we mess up?"

Michael shrugged. "I suppose if we mess up totally, at least whoever we choose will have forgotten about it at the end of the day."

"If we *do* mess up," said Jess, "I guess we can forget about becoming genies, too."

Milly flicked back through the pages. "It's so weird seeing pictures of us—" She broke off. "Hey! This is a new picture. It wasn't here yesterday!"

Jess looked over Milly's shoulder at a picture of her standing in the park with her eyes closed, about to make the wish that brought them home. She read out the caption beneath it: "'Beware of those who watch you.'" She frowned. "What's that supposed to mean?"

"Dunno. What are those shadows there?" asked Jason,

pointing to a pair of tall, dark outlines on the grass behind Jess.

"It must be those policemen." Milly frowned. "Maybe the book means we should watch out for the police?"

Jason looked uncertain. "But I thought the police came up to us from the other side. . . ."

"Forget the shadows," said Michael impatiently. "We passed! We won! We're on to Step Four!"

"I wish we could start after school," Milly said longingly. "But Jason's helping Dad with some trivia questions."

"Too bad, Jase," said Michael. "*I'm* going around to Ben's house after school to spend a few hours on his Megaplay Ultra. . . ."

"You lucky thing!" said Jason.

Milly was disappointed. "I wish we could start Step Four tonight."

"We can always start planning what we're going to do after supper," Jess consoled her.

"That's true." Milly brightened up. "Step Four, already . . . I can't wait!"

After supper, when Mark Worthington had gone to a meeting and Ann was dozing on the couch in the living room, Milly, Jason, Michael, and Jess met in the den.

"You should have been there at Ben's, Jase," said

Michael. "You'd have loved it."

"You didn't ask him," Jess pointed out.

Michael ignored her. "We played Maximum Carnage Two. It's cool. There's all these Slitherbots coming at you and they've got these awesome slush guns—they turn anything they touch into wallpaper paste!"

Milly stifled a yawn.

"Ollie Jones, a boy in my class, has got the Ultra," Jason put in. "He's been going on about how cool Maximum Carnage *Three* is. . . ."

"Then he's talking out of his bum," said Michael, "because that doesn't come out till the autumn."

"He's got a demo version," Jason explained. "His dad works for a software house. Ollie gets early versions of all the latest games."

"*What?*" Michael stared at Jason. "You *know* this kid and you didn't tell me?"

"Is he one of your friends?" Jess asked.

"No way!" Jason pulled a face. "Ollie's got no friends. He's horrible. His mum asked me over to his house during the holidays, remember? I think she hoped we might get on, but he wasn't very nice."

"Who cares if he's *nice*?" Michael cried. "If he gets early versions of the latest games, *I'll* be his friend!"

"I expect even this Ollie has some standards," said Jess.

"And even if he didn't, you wouldn't be able to borrow his games because we don't have anything to play them on," Milly pointed out.

"If Dad still had his old job we could afford an Ultra," said Michael with a sigh.

"But if we get to be real genies we can just wish for one," Jason reminded him.

"Good point," said Michael, brightening. "And if we don't, maybe I could *borrow* good old Ollie's games and play them at Ben's. . . ."

"Never mind about all that," said Milly. "What's our plan with Step Four?"

Skribble popped out of the book. "That is precisely what *I* would like to know!"

"Hi, Skribble!" said Milly.

But the bookworm gave her only the smallest of smiles. "The four of you have wasted an entire day! Now here you are still talking nincompoopy nonsense! Quickly, you must decide. Whom do you choose to be your worthy wish-maker?"

"We could grant a wish for Mum or Mark," Jason suggested. "They're both really deserving."

"Yeah," Milly said excitedly. "We could make the book-shop a mega-success!"

"But only until sunset," Jess pointed out. "And it hasn't even opened yet!"

"Oh." Milly's face fell. "Well, who *can* we grant a wish for, then?"

There was silence as they all considered.

"This Ollie kid!" Michael declared. "Why don't we grant *his* heart's desire?"

"I don't know," said Jason. "The book says the person should be deserving, and Ollie isn't very nice."

"Give him a chance, Jase," Michael said. "Maybe he just doesn't make friends easily . . . like Jess. I'll be genie; I'll take care of it."

Jess glared at him. "You're so transparent, Michael. You only want to go so you can check out what cool stuff he's got, find out what else he likes, then pretend you like it, too, to get in with him!"

"As if!" Michael protested. But he winked at Jason as he said it.

"Actually, Ollie's got a sister about your age, Jess," said Jason. "She was nice. I bet you'd like her—"

"I don't need to be set up with some lame boy's even lamer sister," Jess complained.

"You do," Michael assured her.

"Cease this silly chatter!" Skribble said crossly. "No

147

more delays! Decide!"

"Maybe I *did* get off on the wrong foot with Ollie," said Jason, not wanting to annoy Michael. "He might be all right."

"I can't think of anyone else," Milly admitted. "Jess?"

"Oh, all right," she said. "There's no one in my class I want to grant a wish for. And the sooner we get through Step Four the sooner we become proper genies with proper wishes."

"Sorted, then," said Michael. He looked around at the others. "We'll do it tomorrow, yeah?"

Milly and Jason nodded eagerly, Jess more reluctantly.

"We'll go around to this Ollie's house before school," Michael went on. "We'll leave the lamp where he'll find it, he'll rub it, I'll grant him his wish . . . and we'll all be another step closer to getting our own hearts' desires—just wait!"

Chapter Seventeen

Michael, Milly, Jess, and Jason were all dressed and ready for school by eight o'clock the next morning. The lamp and handbook were stowed safely in Jess's bag. Just to be sure that Ollie knew what to do, Milly had written "rub me" on a label and tied it securely to the lamp's handle.

As they headed to Ollie's house, Jess ran over the final plan they'd decided on: "We get to the house. Michael turns into a genie and then Jason sneaks into the garden, taps on Ollie's window, and leaves the lamp on his windowsill for him to find."

"It would be a lot easier if we could just grant our own wishes again," said Milly.

"This is proper training," Michael reminded her. "It's not supposed to be easy."

"And we can't get ourselves disqualified after all this," Jess added.

"That's Ollie's house," Jason said as they turned into a

wide avenue. "That one with the white door." He pointed out a smart bungalow with large gardens all the way around it. A yard-high wall separated the garden from a narrow path that cut through to the next street. They hurried toward it.

"Ollie's room's that one there," Jason said, pointing to a window that overlooked the path.

Jess looked shiftily about to be sure they weren't being watched, but while one or two commuters were starting up their cars on the avenue, the path was quite secluded. She took *The Genie Handbook* out. There was a rustle and Skribble popped up through a crack in the cover.

"Are we here, at last?" he asked imperiously. "Have you found the boy?"

"Not yet," Michael said. "But any minute now!" He put the lamp on the ground. "Genie me!"

No sooner had he vanished inside than the front door of the bungalow opened and a pretty girl walked out, her chestnut brown hair tied back in a sleek ponytail.

"Get down!" Jess hissed, ducking behind the wall and making Skribble squawk with surprise.

Jason crouched on the pavement beside her. "What is it?"

"You never told me *she* was Ollie's sister!" Jess watched

as the girl walked over to join two other girls with identical ponytails, waiting for her farther up the avenue. "That's Colette Jones and the Colette Clones," Jess whispered as the girls walked away. "They're in my class."

Jason nodded. "I met her when I was here for tea."

"Hurry up, boy!" Skribble interrupted. "Before your wish-maker leaves, too!"

"Here goes!" Picking up the lamp, Jason climbed over the wall and raced across the garden to Ollie's window. He tapped loudly on the glass and then left the lamp on the window ledge. There was a large bush just to one side of the window, and Jason quickly ducked out of sight behind it—as the window opened.

Milly saw Ollie glance out. He had thin, straight brown hair with a fringe that flopped forward and sharp blue eyes that soon fixed upon the lamp on the windowsill.

" 'Rub me,' " Ollie read out. Then he snorted. "Yeah, right. As if! It's bound to be a trick or something." He stuck his head out the window and yelled: "Well, ha, ha, ha, whoever you are. You've lost your lamp, you big losers!"

Then the window slammed shut with a bang.

Inside the lamp, Michael felt the world turn upside down. "Whoa!" he cried, crashing into the metal sides as Ollie chucked the lamp across his bedroom. It landed with a thud.

"What kind of nut do they take me for?" Michael heard Ollie's voice above him. "It's not like I'm some dumb little kid who believes in magic!"

Michael jumped to his feet. "Rub the lamp!" he yelled. He banged on the sides. "Pick it up and rub it!" But Ollie didn't seem to hear. There was the sound of footsteps moving away and then a door slamming shut. Then there was silence.

"Oh, great," Michael groaned, shoving his head in his hands. "*Now* what am I going to do?"

Outside, Jason had raced back to join the others. "The plan's gone wrong!" he gasped, scrambling over the wall. "Ollie thinks it's a trick and won't rub the lamp!"

"We heard," said Milly worriedly. "So Michael's stuck!"

"He could be there till sunset," Jess realized.

"Or a good deal longer," said Skribble.

"What do you mean?" Jason asked.

"As you know, a genie cannot leave his lamp until someone rubs it," the bookworm reminded them. "The wishes that trainee genies grant only last until sunset. But the genie form is much stronger magic, granted by the book, and will last until the genie is summoned."

Milly stared at him in dismay. "So Michael could be stuck in Ollie's house forever unless we get the lamp back?"

"Or until the lamp is rubbed," Jason realized.

"But what if Ollie throws it in the bin?" Tears welled up in Milly's eyes. "We'll never see Michael again!"

"You really are the most incompetent clutch of children!" railed Skribble. "Whatever possessed you to choose someone who wouldn't rub the lamp? Of all the ridiculous things to do!"

"How were we to know Ollie would think it was a trick?" said Jess.

"Can't you help us, Skribble?" Milly begged.

"There is nothing I can do," said Skribble, more softly.

Jess glanced at her watch and groaned. "Look at the time! We're late for school and . . . Quick, *duck*!" She yanked them both down behind the wall as Ollie came out of the front door and slouched away down the drive.

"Never mind school," said Milly fiercely. "We've got to get Michael out!"

"We can't just break in, can we?" Jess said. "And if our schools phone home to find out why none of us are there . . . Look. We'll come back straight after school when Ollie's here and ask for the lamp back, okay?"

Milly carefully closed *The Genie Handbook* and put it in her schoolbag. "He'd just better say yes. . . ."

Inside the lamp, Michael was pacing around in a small circle. "How am I going to get out of here?" he shouted. His voice echoed back at him mockingly from the brass walls of his prison.

The others will come and get me, Michael told himself. He sat down and leaned against the wall of the lamp. "Wish I had my Game Boy with me. Still, I won't be here long."

Two hours later, he realized that his optimism was misplaced.

Three hours later, he realized the lamp was not equipped with a toilet.

By midday, he had worked out his 133rd preferred method of taking a terrible revenge on Milly and his stepsiblings.

By one o'clock he'd decided he would give them anything in the world if they would only get him out of here.

And by three thirty, Michael was going out of his mind with boredom. His stomach felt as if a wolf was tearing at it from the inside. He hadn't had anything to eat since breakfast and that had only been half a piece of toast.

"Please, guys!" he yelled in desperation. "This is officially *not* fun anymore. I'm a genie—get me out of here!"

Chapter Eighteen

Even as Michael yelled for help, Milly and Jason were crouched outside behind the wall, waiting for Jess— and for Ollie.

"Here he comes," hissed Milly as Ollie came sauntering up the drive to his front door and let himself in. "Jase, you know him—ask him to give us the lamp back."

"At once!" came Skribble's muffled voice from the book in Milly's schoolbag.

"Okay," said Jason. He walked up the drive as casually as he could and knocked on the door.

Ollie opened it. "Oh, it's you, Jason," he said shortly. "What do you want?"

"I . . . I wondered if you had seen a lamp lying around." Jason felt the words tumble out of him. "Some people are looking for it on the next street and I said I'd help them find it."

"Who are they?" Ollie demanded.

"I, er, don't know," Jason said quickly. "If you've got

the lamp, I'll go and give it back to them, and find out who they are."

"Well, I *haven't* got it," said Ollie.

"Yes, you have," said Jason. "We . . . *they* saw you pick it up."

"So why are they looking on the next street, then?" Ollie inquired.

"I . . ." Jason blinked. "I don't know," he finished lamely.

"You're such a loser." Ollie shook his head and slammed the door shut.

Jason stared at the shut door for a moment and then walked despondently back down the drive.

"Hey, Jase!" He turned to find Jess hurrying down the avenue. "What did Ollie say?"

As they walked back up the path to where Milly was waiting, Jason explained what had happened. "I told you he was horrible!"

Milly nodded. "He's not a worthy wish-maker at all."

Just then they heard the sound of people walking along the pavement. Jess groaned. "Oh, no, it's Colette!"

"You could ask her to get the lamp," Jason suggested.

"But I hardly know her!" Jess cringed. "I can't just go up and start asking about some stupid lamp. She'll spread it all over school tomorrow. Everyone will laugh at me!"

"Would you like me to come with you?" Milly offered.

"That'll only make it worse!" Jess buried her face in both hands. If she had to get into Colette's house, the last thing she wanted was her kid sister hanging around. *Stepsister,* she corrected herself. "Just stay here, both of you." Jess got up and marched toward the house.

Colette was just putting her key into the door.

"Hi, Colette!" Jess called out in a shaky voice.

Colette turned around. "Oh, hi . . . Jess." She shrugged. "What do you want?"

"I . . . um . . . I saw you and I . . ." Jess's mind raced for a good excuse. "I was just wondering if you'd written down tonight's science homework?"

Colette looked puzzled. "It was just to finish off writing up the experiment, remember? Nothing complicated."

"Oh, yeah. Dumb of me to forget." Jess cursed herself for not thinking of something better, but it was too late now. "I'll . . . I'll just go then, I guess."

Colette looked at her for a moment and then smiled. "Do you want to come in? We could do some of our homework together."

Jess stared at her. Was this a trick? Or was Colette Jones, the most popular girl in her class, actually being friendly?

"Well?" asked Colette.

"I'd love to," Jess murmured shyly. "Thanks."

Colette opened the door. "Come on, then!"

Glancing over her shoulder, Jess saw Milly pop up from behind the fence, giving her a thumbs-up. "Go away!" Jess mouthed frantically. *Colette's going to think I'm teaching my little sister how to stalk her or something!*

She followed Colette into a hallway. It was smartly decorated in shades of white and pale brown. An open door led into an enormous lounge. Jess caught a glimpse of two dark brown leather sofas, and a huge plasma TV on the wall. Colette headed out of the hall and along a wide corridor. There was a spacious designer kitchen on one side and bedrooms on the other. One door, half open, had Colette's name on a china plaque with painted stars around it. The other, firmly shut, had a handmade notice with the words: OLLIE'S ROOM. STRICTLY PRIVATE! written on it.

Jess couldn't resist looking inside Colette's bedroom. She felt a twinge of jealousy at how lovely it was, neat and tidy with purple walls framed by a sparkling white ceiling and carpet. There was a white dresser with a large double bed at one side, and hanging from the ceiling was a set of wind chimes with delicate glass fairies, tinkling in the breeze from the open window.

Fairies?

Jess stared. She had never expected to see fairies in Colette Jones's bedroom. Her gaze fell on the bookcase by the window. The bottom shelf was filled with many of the same books she had had when she was younger— books about enchanted forests, unicorns, and mermaids. *I'd never have thought Colette was the sort of person who was into magic when she was little,* Jess thought.

Suddenly she gasped. There by the open window was Milly!

"Have you got the lamp yet?" Milly whispered.

"I'm working on it!" Jess said in a low voice. "Go away before you ruin everything!" With that, she hurried after Colette, who was in the kitchen pouring them each a glass of orange juice.

"I like the wind chimes in your room," said Jess shyly.

"Oh, that old thing." Colette looked a bit embarrassed. "I should take it down. Fairies are so babyish, aren't they?"

"Well, yeah, of course they are, but even so . . ." Jess smiled self-consciously. "I really like it."

"You do?" Colette looked at her. "My mum's always telling me it's babyish. She's got this interior designer from Oxford making me a glass mobile to hang in its place."

"Wow," said Jess. But Colette didn't look so excited. *She probably has tons of cool stuff like that coming her way,* Jess thought.

"Were you into magic and stuff when you were

younger?" Colette asked hesitantly.

"Kind of." Jess decided to be cool. "When I was really little."

"Me too," said Colette.

Jess wondered what Colette would say if she told her the truth about why she was *really* there—that she had come to rescue her stepbrother who was stuck in a magic lamp, trapped in the form of a bearded genie in a ninja outfit! "So where shall we do our homework?" she asked, changing the subject.

Colette started taking her books out. "We can do it in here. Mum and Dad are both working late, so there's just my little brother, and he'll probably be playing video games in the lounge." She pulled a face. "He's such a pain. Do you have brothers and sisters?"

"A brother, a stepbrother, *and* a little stepsister," Jess said. She glanced nervously at the kitchen window, half expecting Milly to come popping up with a set of binoculars.

"Three of them!" Colette's eyes widened. "That's gruesome. How do you cope?"

"Barely!" Jess shrugged. "I'm just, like, 'whatever . . .'"

Colette smiled and nodded. "I wish I had an older brother instead."

Jess raised her eyebrows. "One with cute mates?"

"Naturally!" Colette replied with a grin. "So, you're new around here—where did you move from . . . ?"

As the conversation went on, Jess felt herself start to relax. This was fun. Almost like being back with her old friends, just chatting and hanging out after school. But at the back of her mind was the thought of Michael. *I have to rescue him,* she reminded herself.

Just then she heard a door open and saw Ollie slouch along the corridor toward the lounge. Her heart thudded. Maybe now was her chance. "Um, can I use your loo?" she asked Colette as casually as she could.

"Sure," Colette replied. "It's just down the hall, past Ollie's room."

Perfect. Jess left the kitchen. Ollie's door was shut, and she could hear the TV blaring in the lounge.

Fingers shaking, she turned Ollie's door handle and slipped into the room. The smell of sweat and old sneakers hit her. Plastered over the pale blue walls were posters of comic book characters, and on the desk near the window a war game had been set up with small plastic aliens. Her eyes swept over the floor, which was covered with a clutter of clothes, toys, and gaming magazines. Where was the lamp? Her heart quickened as she caught a glimpse of gold beneath some old socks.

Jess flew across the room. "Got you!" she breathed,

bending down to grab the lamp.

"What are *you* doing in my room?" An accusing voice made her jump. She swung around. Ollie was scowling in the doorway.

"Er . . . nothing!" Jess stammered. She felt a blush blaze over her face. "I . . . I was just trying to find the toilet."

"No, you weren't," said Ollie. "You were after that lamp, weren't you? You were about to pick it up when I came in."

Then, with the worst timing in the world, Colette appeared in the doorway. "What's going on?"

"I—I got the wrong door," Jess stammered.

"Yeah, right!" Ollie jabbed a finger at her. "You were trying to nick that lamp. The one that was left on my windowsill."

"Don't be stupid," Colette said witheringly to Ollie. "As if Jess would be after anything of yours."

"Yeah." Jess hastily joined Colette by the door. "As if I would!"

"Bet you *were* trying to get it." Ollie picked up the lamp. "What is it with this thing?"

"It looks just like a magic lamp from a fairy story." Colette smiled suddenly. "I've always wished I could find one of those."

"Really?" Jess said in surprise.

Colette blushed. "Um . . . I mean I *used* to wish it. When I was a really little kid, of course." She swung around, looking suddenly flustered. "Come on! What are we doing here, wasting our time in Ollie's freak pit? Oh, yeah—you need the toilet. It's next door."

Slipping into the bathroom, Jess locked the door and groaned. Now Colette must think she was a total weirdo, too stupid to find her way past two doors to a bathroom, and she'd blown her only chance of getting to Michael. Things were not going well—they were not going well at all!

"Jess!" Michael shouted. "Is that you?" Surely he had heard her voice?

Suddenly the lamp rocked, and he was hurled all about it.

"I suppose I might get a few quid for this if I flogged it to a junk shop." That was Ollie's voice, loud and clear—he had to be looking at the lamp up close. "Mind you, needs a polish . . ."

"Yes!" Michael urged the boy, realizing this was his chance. "Yes, yes, yes, yes—*WHOA!*"

With a sudden, sooty *whoosh* of smelly air, Michael was catapulted out of the lamp. He gasped and collapsed in front of the door, clutching at his legs.

"Huh? Who—where—how . . . ?" Ollie, a skinny streak of nothing with a pointy face, looked petrified. "What . . . ?"

"Cramp," groaned Michael. "I've been bunched up in there for—"

Ollie yelled at the top of his lungs.

"What's up with you now, Ollie?" Michael heard a girl's voice call. *Must be Ollie's sister,* he realized. *Guess that's who I heard.*

"Don't tell her I'm here," Michael warned Ollie, his genie voice rumbling up inside him. "Or you will regret it!"

"It's n-n-n-nothing, Colette!" Ollie called, looking warily at Michael. Then he collapsed onto the bed. "This is just a dream, isn't it? I mean, I saw you come out of that lamp. . . ."

While Ollie babbled on, Michael looked around the room. There were some war-gaming figures of Slitherbots with slush guns, there were Manga pictures on the wall . . . and there were CDs strewn over the shelves, review copies and beta versions of all kinds of games. Michael forgot all about his hunger pains.

"Hey!" Ollie gasped. "*Now* I get it. You're a *genie*!"

"What is your heart's desire?" boomed Michael. "Mate," he added.

"I . . ." Ollie frowned. "I dunno. This is like . . . a dream."

How original, thought Michael. "Something to do with games, maybe?"

"I'm already bored with the Ultra. . . ." Ollie looked suddenly thoughtful. "What I'd *really* like is a console that no one else has got. Something so cool it'll prove I'm way better than everyone else." His eyes gleamed. "Yeah, that's my wish, Genie! I want to play a version of Maximum Carnage that's super-real—as real as real life!"

You what? thought Michael. But already, flash-frames of Maximum Carnage game-play were zapping through his mind and big, booming words were rising up in his throat. "Your wish is my command!" he roared, loud enough to shake the windows.

Then there was silence.

Ollie looked around. "Well? Where is it then?"

Michael frowned. The wish had been a vague one, and he hadn't been sure how to grant it. Had it come true?

"If you've messed up, I'll—I'll sue you," snarled Ollie, hands on hips. "Hand it over!"

"*Help!*" came a shriek from outside the bedroom.

"That's Jess!" Michael muttered. He threw open the bedroom door. . . .

To find a huge, horrifying Slitherbot from Maximum

Carnage blocking his way. It looked like a half-melted marrow on legs, glaring at him through oily red eyes. But this was no creature of pixels and imagination. It was a living, breathing, snarling, spitting, scaly, slimy real-life monster.

And it was pointing its slush gun straight at him. . . .

Chapter Nineteen

Back outside, Milly jumped as *The Genie Handbook* started to shake in her hands.

"My tail!" squawked Skribble, squirming about inside the book. "Magic is being drawn into the house."

"Then Michael's out of the lamp!" Jason realized.

"Jess did it!" cried Milly with delight.

Then they heard the shouts for help, and a strange, gruff, grunting noise.

Jason gulped. "But *what* did she do?"

"Wow, that's amazing!" breathed Ollie. Pushing Michael aside, he strode up to the Slitherbot and yanked away its weapon before it could react. "This slush gun is so detailed. . . . Impressive 3-D render, Genie!"

Michael gulped as the monster glared down at Ollie and took a squelching step toward him.

"It's all so lifelike!" Ollie raised the gun and fired, and the monster suddenly splurged away into thick green dribbles.

He grinned in delight. "Or do I mean, *death*like!"

Michael was already jumping across the molten remains of the monster and out into the corridor, his heart pounding. "Hey, Jess!" he shouted. "You okay?"

"No!" he heard Jess yell back. But he couldn't see her for the two enormous Slitherbots advancing on the kitchen. . . .

"Quick," Michael gasped, terrified, "while those things have got their backs turned!" He grabbed the slush gun off Ollie. It felt very real and surprisingly light, just the way he'd always imagined it would if *he'd* been the hero in the game. He heard a girl scream. The monsters had reached the kitchen doorway!

Michael lifted the gun and took aim. *Now!*

As he pulled the trigger, a bolt of yellow light blasted out. With a wet thud, both monsters exploded into slush. Green goo splattered the pristine walls of the hallway.

Now that the monsters had gone, Michael could see Jess in the kitchen comforting a dark-haired girl who was sobbing against her shoulder.

"Hey, give me that slush gun!" Ollie dropped the lamp and yanked the weapon away from Michael. "You only grant the wishes; *I'm* the one who has all the fun!"

"You don't get it, Ollie!" Michael swung around hotly. "I think I made this game *too* real—"

He broke off with a gasp as another Slitherbot marched out of the lounge. Before Michael could do anything to stop it, it had grabbed Ollie by the back of the neck and lifted him into the air. The boy cried out and struggled, dropped the gun, and the Slitherbot threw him against the wall.

"H-h-h-help!" squeaked Ollie as he landed in a sprawling heap.

"Wish them away!" Michael boomed. "Wish them *away*, you idiot, *now*!"

But Ollie was lost in a blind panic. Grabbing the fallen lamp, he struggled to his feet, raced to the front door, threw it open, and ran outside. Meanwhile, Michael lunged for the gun. If he could only slush the Slitherbot . . .

But just before he could reach it, his genie slippers began to glow—and suddenly he found himself being pulled toward the front door. He tried to stop and turn back for the slush gun, but it was no good.

It must be the lamp, he realized as he barged past the Slitherbot. *There's a link between genie and lamp—and after what happened in London, if the lamp's going one way, I guess I have to follow. . . .*

The Slitherbot picked up the slush gun from the floor. Now it had one in each hand. It glowered at Michael, gave a deep roar, and aimed them both straight at him. . . .

"*Genie me again!*" Michael shouted in terror, just in time. As the slush guns fired, he felt himself being whisked through the air after Ollie and spiraling back inside the lamp.

"Jess, hang in there," Michael gasped. "I'll sort it out. I'll make everything okay. . . ."

Yeah, sure you will, hero, he thought bitterly. *But how?*

Jason and Milly could hear all the commotion from outside the house.

"Oh, Skribble, what's going on?" asked Milly.

"My dear child," Skribble sighed, "I cannot see through walls!"

"You don't have to," said Jason. "Look!"

Ollie had burst out of the front door, clutching the lamp. He ran across the garden as if his life depended on it. A cloud of dark smoke suddenly spiraled after him, and vanished into the lamp's spout.

"That was Michael!" Milly slammed the handbook shut, making Skribble yelp with fright, and pelted off down the path after the disappearing Ollie. "You check on Jess. Be careful!"

Jason nodded and ran inside the house. "Jess?" he called anxiously. "Jess, where are you? Are you—"

The door slammed shut behind him. He broke off and whirled around. . . .

To find himself face-to-face with a big, green monster. He recognized it at once—a Slitherbot, brought to gruesome, full-size life. And that gun . . . Jason remembered Michael banging on about them in the den the night before. *The rays turn anything they touch into wallpaper paste. . . .*

He opened his mouth to yell, but someone else beat him to it.

"Jason, get in here!" screamed Jess, sticking her head out of a room farther down the long hallway.

Jason didn't stop to think twice. He ran toward her.

"We're going to block ourselves in Colette's bedroom!" She grabbed his arm and yanked him inside—just as the Slitherbot behind him opened fire. The blast went wide, hit a coat stand in the hall, and turned it into wood-textured trickles.

Colette slammed the door shut and started dragging her dressing table over to barricade it.

"Thanks," squeaked Jason as he sank, shaking, to the floor.

"Where's Milly?" demanded Jess. "Is she okay?"

"She's gone after Ollie to get Michael and the lamp back."

"What *is* it with this lamp?" Colette wailed. "What's

going on? Where did *you* spring from?"

"Uh . . . just called around to see Ollie," said Jason, suddenly remembering their vow to keep everything secret, whatever happened. If Jess hadn't told Colette what was going on, then neither could he.

"Come on, Jase," said Jess, "help me move the bed in front of the door." She lowered her voice. "Ollie must have wished these monsters could come out of his dumb video game. What an idiot!"

"The good news is they'll vanish at sunset," said Jason, straining to shift the bed.

"The bad news is, that's still an hour away," Jess pointed out. "You've seen what their guns can do and you know what Skribble said yesterday—'the effects of the magic will remain.'"

Jason stared at her. "So whoever gets slushed, *stays* slushed?"

Jess felt sick. "Yes."

"What are you two going on about?" Colette said, pushing her hands through her hair. "What's going on?"

Before they could answer, the top of the bedroom door burst apart like a water bomb. Colette shrieked.

"We'll never last till sunset!" cried Jason. "What are we going to do?"

* * *

172

Milly panted for breath as she ran after Ollie, forcing herself to keep going. But his legs were longer than hers, and her schoolbag slung over one shoulder was slowing her down.

"Retrieve the lamp, Milly!" she heard Skribble cry. "Free your bothersome brother from this odious Ollie's control so he can put things right!"

But Ollie was getting away. *I need to get his attention,* Milly realized, staggering to a stop. *Time for a bit of improvising . . .*

"Oliver Jones!" she bellowed with the last of her breath.

Her shout echoed around the quiet street, so loudly that Ollie actually stopped running. Then he frowned and looked about. "Where . . . where did my genie go?"

"I'm glad you finally noticed," said Milly, desperately trying not to seem out of breath as she walked toward him. "I am your genie's personal assistant. He's been called away by the, uh, League of Genies . . . on urgent magic business."

"Hang on." Ollie scowled. "I recognize you. You're from my school."

"Duh! I'm in disguise!" Milly rolled her eyes and walked right up to him, lowering her voice. "Now, hear my words, Oliver Jones. It is easy to get your genie to come back to you when he's been tied up on magic business." She smiled innocently. "You simply say, 'Genie be free.'"

"I see. . . ." Ollie nodded to himself. "Well, I want him here now—*Genie be free!*"

There was a squall of black smoke as Michael shot out of the lamp in his normal form. But before Ollie could see anything clearly, Milly belted him as hard as she could with her schoolbag. With a squawk of surprise, Ollie fell down in a heap on the pavement. Milly snatched the lamp from him, and then Michael grabbed her by the arm and they ran off back toward the house.

"Nice going, sis," said Michael. "But now you'd better get into the lamp quick, in case Ollie comes after us and recognizes you. Besides, it'll be the safest place."

"What do you mean?" panted Milly.

"Jess and Colette are in big trouble. There are real Slitherbots in the house, with working slush guns!"

"What?" Milly gasped. "I sent Jason inside to check that Jess was okay!"

"Oh, fantastic. Come on!" As Milly sent herself into the lamp, Michael put on an extra burst of speed. *But what am I going to do when I get there?* he thought. *What?*

Chapter Twenty

Jason stared in horror as the Slitherbots blasted the door again. The wood burst into torrents of brown water. Now he could see the monsters' hideous green faces, the crimson of their narrowed eyes.

"They're going to get in!" he shouted, terrified. "There's nothing we can do to stop them!"

The Slitherbots growled and prepared to fire at the dresser blocking their way. Colette shrieked. Jess jumped onto the big bed as she hurried to get away, and bumped her head on the fairy wind chimes. They clanged and tinkled around her ears.

In desperation, she tugged them down from the ceiling and hurled them at the nearest Slitherbot. They tangled around his head and he howled in anger. The more he shook his head, the more the chimes jangled, enraging and distracting both him and the monsters behind him. They clawed at the delicate glass fairies with their sticky, spongy hands.

"Come on," gasped Colette. "The window—maybe we can get out in time." She ran over to her bedroom window—just as Michael burst into view. With a scream of surprise she jumped back.

"Hey, I'm one of the good guys!" Michael protested, grabbing Colette's hand. He helped her clamber out into the garden.

"Good guy?" Jess snorted, helping Jason through, then scrambling after him. "This is all *your* fault, Michael!"

"Huh?" Colette stared between the two of them, confused. "What's going on?"

"This is Michael, our stepbrother," Jason explained.

"Everything's *always* my fault around here," said Michael sourly, leading the charge across the grass toward the wall, Milly's schoolbag bouncing around on his back.

"Michael, how did you get out?" Jess hissed so Colette wouldn't hear her.

"Milly got me out of Ollie's control and now she's in the lamp," said Michael, patting his jacket pocket. "About the safest place right now."

"Then let's wish our way out of this!"

"Duh!" Michael retorted. "The book said we couldn't grant each other's wishes, remember? We'll get disqualified—no more genie training."

Jess buried her face in her hands. "No more *anything* if

we don't get rid of those things!"

"The house!" Colette shrieked, looking back over her shoulder. "Look!" Sections of the brickwork were starting to dissolve into water as the aliens attempted to blast their way out of her bedroom.

As they reached the garden wall, Jason turned to Michael. "Colette has to wish them away and put everything back as it was. It's our only chance."

"And, like, *now*," Michael agreed, pulling the lamp from his pocket and shoving it into Colette's hands. "Do it!"

The girl stared at the lamp, bewildered. "I'm asleep," she murmured, falling to her knees on the grass. "That must be it. This is all a nightmare."

Jess grabbed hold of Colette by the shoulders and spoke in a low, urgent voice. "Colette, listen. You know we were talking about magic before, and how we used to believe in it when we were little? Well, it really does exist!"

Colette stared at her.

"I know it seems crazy, like kid stuff," Jess went on desperately. "I know everyone thinks magic is babyish but . . . this whole mess is because of magic. And only magic can put it right!"

"They're coming!" howled Jason as four huge Slitherbots lumbered into sight through the hole in the wall.

"Oh, Jess," Colette gasped. "I've always wanted to believe in magic. . . ." Her eyes widened. "You're not tricking me? It's really real?"

"You'll have the proof when those things blast us to bits," Michael growled. "Now, *rub the lamp!*"

The green, glutinous monsters stomped toward the garden wall.

"Hurry!" cried Skribble from inside Milly's schoolbag.

"Colette?" Jess said urgently. "What's your heart's desire?"

Colette rubbed the lamp hard. "I wish this craziness had never started," she cried fervently, "and that things were back the way they were!"

Milly blew out of the lamp in a blur of gold trousers and a strappy red top. Her turban was glittering with gold sequins, and her eyes were elaborately made up in gold and black to disguise her appearance. Jason gazed at her, seriously impressed—then yelled as the Slitherbots loomed up behind her.

Milly turned to face them, unafraid. "As you wish it," she boomed, in a voice that thundered up to the skies above, "*so shall it be!*"

The Slitherbots defiantly lifted their slush guns to fire at her, at Colette—at *all* of them. . . .

And then they vanished.

The garden was silent and peaceful once more. For a long moment, nobody moved. Then Jason slowly raised his head and started peering all around.

"It's okay," Milly told him in a whisper that sounded like distant thunder. "They've gone."

Jess punched the air. "It's over!"

Michael turned to Milly and grinned. "You did it."

Milly looked like she might burst with happiness. "I couldn't have done it without Colette!" she said, pirouetting as she shrank back into the lamp. "See you later, guys!" With that, she vanished down the brass spout.

Michael gently took the lamp from Colette's hands. "Say, 'Genie be free,'" he told her.

"Genie be free," she repeated, parrot fashion. Colette was so deep in a daze she didn't even notice as Milly burst out of the spout in her school uniform and flew right over a bush, landing in a noisy heap.

Michael placed the lamp inside Milly's schoolbag, next to the handbook. Then he handed the bag to Milly. "Stay here," he murmured. "The less she knows the better, yeah?"

"Okay," sighed Milly. "I'll wait with Skribble."

Colette was staring at the holes in the wall of her house. "The wish hasn't worked completely. What will Mum and Dad say when—"

"Give it a chance," said Jess, putting a sympathetic hand on her shoulder. "That was quite a big wish you asked for."

Colette looked at her with wide eyes. "You're, like, an expert at this, aren't you?"

Jess blushed. "Not really."

"None of us are," sighed Michael.

"Look!" Jason pointed at the side of the house. The holes in the wall were fading away to leave perfect brickwork in their place.

Taking a deep, shaky breath, Colette headed toward the house. "Okay. Let's go inside and check the place out." She ran to the front door and pushed it open, Michael, Jess, and Jason following her.

"The coat stand's come back," Jason noted. "That's a good sign."

Just then, the door to Ollie's room opened and he wandered out.

"Ollie!" gasped Jason. "Where did you spring from?"

"I live here, you idiot!" Ollie frowned. "And if you've come to hang out with me, tough. I'm busy."

"He didn't come to see *you*, moron," said Michael, taking an angry step toward Ollie. "However many cool games you might have."

Ollie scowled at his sister. "Keep your weirdo friends

out of the lounge, Colette." He yawned. "I want to go on the Ultra later and I'm *not* sharing."

"Thank goodness!" sighed Jason, and the others all shared knowing looks. Infuriated, Ollie slammed his door shut on them, and they burst into laughter.

"Come on, Colette," said Jess. "Let's check your room."

Colette led the others into her bedroom. Everything was back to normal—the door, the bed, the fairy chimes, all perfectly in place.

"Magic," breathed Colette. "Proper magic." She grinned at Jess. "It really exists!"

Michael groaned. "Oh, you two aren't going to start that again, are you? Come on, Jase. Let's scope out the rest of the place. Make sure it really *is* Slitherbot-free."

"But it will be," said Jason. "The magic will have worked."

"I still think we should go and check." Michael jerked his head toward Colette and Jess and gave Jason a meaningful look. "Maybe start in the lounge?"

Understanding dawned on Jason's face. "Oh, yeah, yeah," he said quickly. "We should definitely go and check."

Together, they went out, leaving Jess and Colette alone. Colette looked at the shelf of books about mermaids and unicorns and enchanted princesses.

"It's funny how I could never bear to throw those books away," she said. "I guess I didn't want to stop believing in magic." She looked at Jess. "So what other magic have you done? Tell me about it!"

Jess hesitated. But then she remembered that at sunset, as the worthy wish-maker, Colette would forget everything.

And so Jess started talking. She told Colette about the handbook and about the adventures they'd had, about Jason getting stuck in the lamp, about the fuss with the food and the trip to London. Colette listened, wide-eyed.

"Oh, wow," she breathed. "It's crazy; it's so way out and . . . and *ridiculous*!"

Jess smiled. "I suppose it is!"

Colette smiled back. "You're amazing, Jess. I've always wished I could have a friend who was more like me. I've got loads of mates but none of them would dare to talk about believing in magic in case they got laughed at. You're way cool."

Jess was very pleased but also embarrassed. "Nah. You've got it wrong." She pointed to a pair of strappy red sandals with killer heels by the dresser. "What's *way* cool are those shoes!"

They both laughed. "Do you want to try them on?" Colette offered.

"Can I?" said Jess eagerly, slipping them onto her feet. They were a perfect fit.

"I'll never forget today." Colette shook her head. "Never."

Jess felt a twinge of guilt. *Oh, yes, you will,* she thought.

"Guess we'd better finish our homework now." Colette went to the door. "From magic lamps and monsters to scattering light through prisms—what a comedown." She paused. "Actually, maybe after all the excitement, it'll be good to get back to something totally boring and normal!"

Jess grinned and followed her toward the kitchen, but then she heard the sound of gunfire from the lounge.

Heart thumping, she looked around the door—to find Jason and Michael sitting in front of the wall-mounted TV, yanking on joysticks and giving the fire buttons a good thumb pummeling. "What are you doing?" she exclaimed.

Michael hit PAUSE and looked up innocently. "Just checking that no Slitherbots are going to come out of Ollie's Ultra at us!"

"Uh-huh." Jess smiled wearily. "Very thorough." Then she glanced out the window and realized that the sun was close to setting. When the book had done its work, would

Colette remember that the two of them had talked at all, that she had shared her secret longing to believe in magic? Or would she just think Jess was a weirdo trying to steal her shoes?

Leaving the boys to their game, Jess went into the kitchen. She sat down and stared nervously at her homework.

"Are you okay?" Colette frowned. "You look . . ." She broke off as the last curve of the sun sank behind the hills, and put her hands to her forehead. "Oh! That's funny, I . . . I was going to say . . ."

Jess looked at her anxiously. "Colette?"

"Sorry, my head feels strange, all kinds of swirly. . . . Must be this dumb homework sending me to sleep!" Colette shook her head and sighed. "Don't you wish, sometimes, that something really exciting would happen?"

Jess almost burst into hysterical laughter. "Yeah . . . sometimes." She heard the soft click of the front door opening as Michael and Jason slipped away into the night, and decided to risk it. "Sometimes I wish that something *magical* would happen. It would be fun to believe in magic . . . wouldn't it?"

"Yes," said Colette. "It would be brilliant."

They grinned at each other. Jess got up. "I suppose I should be getting back home."

"Hey, my shoes look great on you," Colette noticed.

"You should have them."

Jess stared. "What? But I can't just keep them! They're much too expensive!"

"They're too tight on me." Colette waved away her protests. "And I've got loads of other shoes. I'm glad you came around," she went on as they walked into the hall. "I've really enjoyed it—just sitting and chatting. . . ."

Sitting and chatting! Jess had to hide her smile. "I've really enjoyed myself, too." She paused. "Wait a sec. I think I left my other shoes in your room."

She hurried into Colette's bedroom. The fairy wind chimes tinkled gently. Jess touched one of the little glass figures and smiled, remembering something else the book had said about the wish-maker.

"He will surely come to know happiness," she whispered. "Or *she* will, anyway."

Picking up her old shoes, she went back to the hall. She said good-bye to Colette, then turned and set off into the chilly evening. Her feet were a little cold in the sandals, but inside she felt warmer than she had for ages.

Chapter Twenty-one

Jason, Michael, and Milly were waiting for Jess on the path.

"Everything all right?" asked Jason.

"Everything's great," Jess replied. "But now let's get home."

"I wonder what the book says." Milly reached into her bag as they set off along the avenue. "I've been dying to look."

She opened the book. Skribble was lurking near the front of Step One. "Is all well now, Milly?"

"I think so." Milly looked at Michael and wrinkled her nose. "But I have to say, it was *very* stinky in that lamp."

Michael blushed. "I was stuck inside for about seven hours. I was bursting! Where was I *supposed* to go?"

"Gross!" wailed Jess as Jason sniggered.

"You foolish youth," Skribble chided. "Why did you not simply say the genie Time Twisting spell?"

They looked blankly at him.

Skribble tutted. "It is basic genie training! Some genies

have to wait in their lamp for centuries before a wish-maker comes along. How d'you think *they* manage, eh?" He shook his head. "They utter the Time Twisting spell and it's as if only a single moment has passed between their vanishing into the lamp and their next appearance."

Michael groaned. "Now he tells us!"

"It was there in the introduction to the book all along," Skribble railed, "if only you had taken the time to—"

Jess was peering at the page in the introduction. "There are *some* words here. . . . 'Time turn. Time twist—.'" She looked pointedly at Skribble. "The rest of the page has been nibbled away to nothing."

Skribble held dead still. "Don't be preposterous, girl!" he snapped. "Why, the spell in its entirety is quite clearly spelled out . . . er . . ."

"You *ate* that spell and didn't even bother to tell us about it?" Michael's eyes narrowed. "So all that time I was stuck in the lamp with my bladder about to explode, starving hungry, out of my mind with boredom—if I'd known the spell I could have switched myself off just . . . like . . . that?"

Skribble fixed him with a haughty look. "You had simply to say: 'Time turn. Time twist. Make the hours pass like this!'" He slapped his tail against the page and made a sound like a whip crack. "Although since you don't possess a tail, you would have to click your fingers." The bookworm puffed himself up to full, not-very-impressive height. "If you had only asked of my great wisdom . . ."

"Worm!" Michael roared. "I'm really, *really* gonna squash you this time!" He lunged for the book as Skribble disappeared hastily inside its pages. Jason grabbed Michael around the waist to hold him back as Milly scampered away, holding the book out of reach.

"It's all right," Milly said soothingly to the empty page. "Michael will calm down soon."

Then Jess gave a sudden gasp of alarm.

Milly looked up and followed her gaze. Two people were hovering at the end of the avenue in the orange glow of a street lamp. The man was tall and skinny with smooth black hair, a razor-sharp moustache, and dark eyes. The woman beside him was slender and wore her black hair in a sleek bob.

Milly felt her skin prickle. "It's the people we saw in the junk shop!" she hissed.

"What're you going on about?" Michael frowned.

"We'll tell you later," Jess whispered. Both the man and the woman were looking straight at them, and Jess had exactly the same creepy feeling as she'd had back in Junk and Disorderly. "Stop mucking around, you lot," she said loudly, grabbing the handbook from Milly. "Give me my library book back and let's go home." She looked warningly at Michael and Jason and muttered, "Turn around and walk the other way. Act natural."

Michael and Jason looked very confused but did as she said.

Jess hustled them toward a path that cut through to the next street. "Come on!" she urged. As soon as they were safely out of sight, she breathed out. "Phew!" She glanced around, half expecting to see the couple coming up behind them, but the path was clear.

"What was all that about?" asked Jason, puzzled.

"We saw that man and woman when we were buying the lamp," Milly said, and she quickly told the boys what had happened in the junk shop. "They gave me a really creepy feeling. You should see their eyes. They're all black and glittery!" She shivered.

"Weird," said Jason.

Michael raised his eyebrows. "You three are the weird ones. What do you think those people are—zombies or something?" He put on a spooky voice and waved his arms over Jess's head. "Whoooo!"

"Stop it!" she said, slapping his hand away. "There's something odd about them. There really is!"

"I hope we don't see them again." Milly shivered. "Come on. Let's go!"

"Get the book open, then," Michael said as soon as they got back to the den. "Let's see what it says. If we've failed this step because I didn't know that stupid Time Twisting spell . . ."

"Let's see. . . ." Jess flicked through the pages.

"There's another picture!" Jason pointed out. "At the end of Step Four!" It showed Colette staring in wonder at her magically mended home.

"What's it say underneath?" said Michael, straining to read.

The Verdict . . .

And thus we see a noble end can be attained through unexpected means. A mistake, once recognized, can be undone so long as the spirit be pure enough and willing.

You have passed Step Four.

"YES!" Michael roared.

"We did it!" Jason cried, grabbing hold of Milly and dancing around in a circle.

Jess gave a happy smile and flung herself onto the sofa.

"That was the scariest day of my life. . . . I can't believe we all came out of it okay *and* we passed!"

"Hang on," Michael called. "Some more words here . . ."

Jason took a look. The words were writing themselves across the page, in larger letters and darker ink. Almost like the book was shouting . . .

AND YET!
Unworthy are they who would seek to use the
spirit and strife of others to achieve their own ends!
Unworthy and fit to be PUNISHED.

"What's all that about?" Michael frowned.

Jess's smile looked a little less certain. "I wish the book was easier to understand."

"Hey, Skribble might know what it means," said Milly. "I wonder where he is. Skribble?" she called softly. No bookworm appeared.

"I can hear him chomping away," said Michael, flicking through to the back of the book. There was Skribble, eating furiously through some picture-filled pages. His cheeks were bulging and his little body looked chunkier than usual.

"Skribble!" Milly said in surprise.

"What are you doing?" asked Jason.

Skribble swallowed a ball of paper so big it made his throat bulge to twice its normal size. "Don't interrupt me when I'm eating! What manners you guttersnipes have." The bookworm looked quite green, but pressed his face back down to the paper. "I must keep eating. Goodness knows what the book's up to, showing such silly pictures . . ."

"What are they pictures of?" Jess said, coming to see. "They're not us."

Milly shook her head. The left-hand page showed two pictures—one of a king looking angry on a throne, and another of a large, fierce-looking genie with a long beard in a room full of books. He seemed to be shaking his fist at something on the right-hand page—but Skribble had chewed the right-hand page almost to nothing.

"Appendix," Jason said, reading some small print on the parchment above the first picture.

"Appendix?" Milly echoed. "Don't you have that taken out in the hospital?"

Jason shook his head. "An appendix is also a collection of extra stuff at the end of a book. It can help you understand the main bit more fully."

"Maybe the book thinks there's something we need to

know," said Jess. "Skribble, stop eating it and let us see."

"No!" Skribble screeched, throwing his body over the page as if trying to hide the pictures.

Milly stared at him in astonishment. "Skribble! This might be important. Anyway, you shouldn't eat so much so quickly; you'll get a tummy ache—"

"Cease your prattling, you ridiculous child!" Skribble pulled himself up to his full height, trembling all over. "How *dare* you address me like a mother does its baby? Leave me alone, d'you hear? *Leave me alone!*"

Milly bit her lip and shrank back into the sofa, her eyes filling with tears. Jess and Jason stared at the bookworm in shock.

"Dumb worm," Michael muttered, putting a hand on his sister's shoulder. "It's all right, Mil. Don't cry."

"I'm not crying," Milly said, sniffing hard.

"Skribble didn't mean it," Jason put in. "Did you, Skribble?"

But with the entire page destroyed in his wake, the bookworm wriggled with some difficulty back inside the book.

Jess patted Milly's arm. "Leave him to it. He'll calm down and say sorry; you'll see."

"Why don't you tell us what we have to do in Step Five,

Milly?" Jason suggested. "You haven't read out from the book yet."

Milly wiped her eyes. "Okay," she said. "I will." She took the book, drew in a deep breath, and began to read in her very best onstage voice. . . .

The Genie Handbook
The Fifth Step:
Beware What You Wish For

YOU WHO ARE WITNESS
TO THESE WORDS!

A worthy wish-maker has now been granted her heart's desire. But as you have discovered to your cost, not all who tread the earth are so deserving of a genie's precious magic. Some people deserve to pay a fitting price for their folly in life, and no good genie will allow them to profit from wish-making.

With this in mind, you must find a subject who deserves to be tricked. He should be a shallow-hearted man, self-serving and self-important. You must hear his wish and, as genie law demands, grant it for him. AND YET! A cunning genie will twist its sense and meaning so that the wish comes true in a most unfortunate manner. . . .

ACT NOT IN HASTE! Others must not suffer from the way in which you grant his wish. Be wary and wise. Failure to achieve success on the first attempt forfeits your right to proceed to the sixth and final step.

YOU HAVE BEEN WARNED.

Chapter Twenty-two

"So we've got to trick someone!" Milly said, putting the book down.

"But if we mess up this time, that's it," noted Michael. "No more genie training. No more magic."

"We'd better think carefully about who we trick, then." Milly looked worried. "Who will it be?"

"Can we think about it tomorrow?" Jason rubbed his head. "I think I've had enough for one day."

"Me too," said Jess. "And I've got loads of history homework to do."

Michael nodded. "Just imagine being able to magic it all away!"

"Let's meet tomorrow and talk about who we'll trick then," said Milly.

Milly and Jason led the way up the stairs. Jess was about to follow them when she noticed the book lying on the sofa and picked it up. "Better put this under Milly's pillow again," she said to Michael. "Skribble's never lost it like that at her before, has he?"

"And it's weird the way he ate that whole page," Michael agreed. "It's like there was something written there that he didn't want us to see. But it was just a picture of some genie in a library. What's the big deal?"

Jess shrugged. "I have absolutely no idea."

"The worm's flipped. That's all it is." He rubbed his hands and set off upstairs. "Time to chill. I may not have an Ultra, but Game Boy, here I come!"

Jason and Milly went through to the lounge. "When's tea going to be?" Milly asked, bouncing down on the sofa next to Ann.

"When your dad has a chance to go get takeout," Ann told her.

"Okay," said Milly, snuggling in beside her.

"Where *is* Mark?" Jason said. "He asked me to test him on some trivia questions tonight."

"He's in the study," said Ann. "But be gentle with him, Jason. I don't think he's feeling too confident!"

Jason went into the study. Mark was sitting in the chair with his eyes closed, a *Fantastic Facts* trivia book lying beside him. "What's the capital of Turkey?" he was muttering. "What is it . . . ?"

"Ankara," Jason said.

Mark jumped. "Oh, hi, Jason." He picked up the book to check. "You're right. Well done." He sighed. "I can't seem to remember anything. These questions are impossible! I mean, what *does* 'http' stand for in website addresses?"

"Hypertext transfer protocol," Jason immediately replied.

"Okay, well, what's half of one third?"

"One sixth," said Jason with a grin.

Mark shook his head in amazement. "You always know the answers. You should be on this trivia team, not me!"

Jason shrugged and took the book from him. "I like trivia questions. Hey, this is a cool one! Is it possible for a man in Scotland to wed his widow's sister?"

"I don't know," Mark said uncertainly. "Maybe there *is* a law about it in Scotland. . . ."

"Mark!" Jason grinned. "It's a trick question! A man can't marry his widow's sister, because if he has a widow it means he must be dead—he can't marry anyone!"

Mark groaned. "I can't manage normal questions, let alone trick ones! Come on, mate, help me with the geography, science, and math ones. Mr. Foxtrot will be livid if I don't get at least some of them right on the night. . . ."

"Who's Mr. Foxtrot?" Jason wondered.

"He's the captain of my trivia team." Mark sighed. "And he takes it all *very* seriously!"

Jason found a geography question. "What's the longest river in the world?"

Mark bit his lip. "Um, the Amazon?"

"Nope, it's the Nile. Here, try another."

Jason asked five geography questions before Mark got one right.

"What am I going to do?" Mark exclaimed. "The Trivia Team Challenge is in two days' time, and I'm going to mess up in front of the whole town! If only there was someone who could take my place—" He broke off and stared at Jason. "Hey! How about you, Jason!"

"Me!" Jason's voice came out in a squeak.

Just then the doorbell rang. "We'll talk about this some more in a minute," Mark said, hurrying out of the study.

"Mr. Foxtrot!" Jason heard him say in surprise as he opened the front door. "I was just talking to Jason about you. What brings you here?"

"Just thought I'd pop 'round," came a voice with a northern accent. "Maybe give you a little extra coaching."

"Well, actually," said Mark, "this is very good timing. I want to talk to you about the trivia challenge. . . ."

Jason poked his head out of the study. Mr. Foxtrot was a large, stocky man whose ruddy cheeks were creased and dimpled with his self-satisfied smile. A pair of chunky glasses had slipped halfway down his bulbous nose. Jason saw that his hair was gray and thinning. Several long strands clung to the big bald patch on top of his head like they'd been glued there. Jason smiled but Mr. Foxtrot's gaze swept over him as if Jason was of no more interest to him than an old piece of furniture.

"Can I get you a coffee?" Mark asked.

"No, no," said Mr. Foxtrot, following Mark into the kitchen. Jason went after them. "So what did you want to talk to me about?"

Mark cleared his throat. "The thing is, Arthur, I really want the team to do well—"

"We shall do more than just well," Mr. Foxtrot interrupted. "I am determined we shall *win*!"

"I know," Mark said slowly. "And because of that . . . I think it might be best if young Jason here swaps places with me."

Mr. Foxtrot stared. "I beg your pardon?"

"He's been testing me on all sorts of questions." Mark smiled. "I know he's only nine, but he's got a great memory for facts."

Mr. Foxtrot swung around and looked Jason up and down incredulously. "Have a child on the team? Ridiculous! We're not running a kindergarten! You just need to practice more, Mark. That's why I've come around. . . ."

Jason wished he could sink through the floor.

Mr. Foxtrot whisked the *Fantastic Facts* book from Jason's hand. "Is this what you're trying to cram from, then, hmm? Bit tatty, isn't it?"

"The information's good," Mark said defensively. "I found it while we were moving shelves around in the shop."

"Hope not all your stock's in this condition; you'll be closed a month after opening!" Mr. Foxtrot chuckled. "No offense meant!"

"None taken," Mark said politely. "We've got some very good books to offer. I hope you'll drop in and see for yourself; we're planning a little opening party on Sunday—"

"Yes, well, I'm a very busy man, of course," Mr. Foxtrot said, not sounding interested. He flicked through the pages of the book and shook his head. "Hardly worth even asking this one, it's so easy, but . . . what is the average of the numbers one, ten, and one hundred?"

Mark looked blank. "Er . . ."

Thirty-seven, thought Jason, working it out. *It's thirty-seven.*

"It's easy," Foxtrot insisted. "Come on."

"Thirty-seven!" Jason blurted out.

Mr. Foxtrot jumped. Then he put down the book crossly. "Reading the answer over my shoulder, were you? That's very rude, young man."

"I wasn't!" Jason protested.

"He doesn't need to," Mark agreed. "I told you Jason was brilliant with facts and figures."

Mr. Foxtrot looked skeptical. "Yes, well. Another question." As he leafed through the pages, Milly came into the kitchen to fix herself a glass of orange juice. She smiled at him, but Mr. Foxtrot ignored her just as he had ignored Jason. "Now then, Mark," he commanded. "What's the name of Pluto's moon?"

"Charon," said Jason, unable to stop himself.

"Sharon?" Mr. Foxtrot spluttered with mirth. "Sharon, he says!"

"Not Sharon, *Charon*," said Jason. "C-H-A . . ."

Foxtrot peered more closely at the fact book and frowned. "Ah. Yes, well, we all knew that, didn't we?" He looked at Mark meaningfully. "You know, in my day, children were seen and not heard!"

Jason blushed and sat down at the table. Milly looked crossly at Mr. Foxtrot.

"Jason was only trying to help," said Mark.

"*I'm* the one who needs help!" Mr. Foxtrot shut the book with a bang. "My team has won the Trivia Team Challenge every year for five years running. I intend to make it *six* years, so I suggest you get studying. We like winners around here, Mark, and we don't have much time for losers." Mr. Foxtrot cleared his throat. "No offense meant. Good night."

Picking up his coat, he marched out of the kitchen.

As Mark followed him stiffly to the front door, Milly looked at Jason. "What a horrid man!" she hissed.

Jason nodded. "You should have seen the look on his face when your dad asked if I could be on the team. He looked at me as if I was a booger or something."

"Poor Dad, having to be bossed around by him," Milly said. "Someone should teach him a lesson." She caught her breath and saw a grin starting on Jason's face. "Oh, Jase! Are you thinking what I'm thinking?"

Jason grinned at her and nodded. "One undeserving subject—delivered straight to our door!"

Chapter Twenty-three

"Hey, Jess! Over here!" Colette called when Jess walked into her classroom the next morning.

"Hi," Jess said shyly.

Colette was sitting on a desk at the back with a group of friends. She got up and went over to Jess. "It was fun last night. You should come over and do your homework again sometime. I mean, if you want to . . . ?"

"That would be great!" said Jess. "And we've got math together after homeroom, haven't we. Maybe we could sit together?"

Colette grinned and nodded. "Maybe we could."

Jess had a much better day at school. She got to know Colette's two best friends, Jodie and Natasha, and found they weren't as clonelike as she'd first thought. Natasha had also moved to Moreways Meet fairly recently; she didn't know many people but she was really into clothes and music. Jodie had five brothers and sisters, so she and

Jess bonded as they moaned about how annoying siblings could be.

After school, Jess walked home with them.

"What are you doing tomorrow afternoon?" Colette asked when they reached Jess's house.

"Yeah, do you want to go shopping with us?" Jodie said. "We're meeting in town."

"I wish I could," Jess replied. "But I've got to go to this trivia thing. Mark, my stepdad, is on one of the teams."

"Never mind," Colette said. "Another time though?"

"Definitely," Jess declared. "See you!"

Just so long as you don't see me *doing genie magic,* she thought. Milly and Jason had told her and Michael about Mr. Foxtrot, and they'd all agreed he seemed the perfect subject to try to trick. They had decided to take the lamp around to his house first thing on Saturday morning.

Jess walked into the house and found her mum in the kitchen.

"You look like you've had a good day," Ann said.

"Yeah," said Jess with a happy sigh. "I have, for a change." She looked around. The house was very quiet. "Where are the others?"

"Milly's gone to see her new friend's pony, Michael's signed up for an after-school karate class, and Jason's at computer club," Ann answered. "It's great that you all seem to be settling in at last."

As Jess headed up to her room she thought about what her mum had said. *Were* they all settling in? Jason seemed more confident in this school than his old one. Michael and Milly had made friends from the start and were joining clubs and finding things to do.

And now maybe I've got friends, too, Jess thought.

So, do I still want to go back to London?

She hesitated.

Yes, she told herself firmly. *I do.*

Jess was just finishing her math homework when Milly bounced in from riding.

"Oh, Jess, I've had the best time!" Milly's grin was so big it almost split her face in two. "Emily and I were taking turns to ride Blaze, her pony; then this friend of Emily's mum called Chris saw us and asked me if I'd like to ride *her* pony. He's called Pepper and Chris's daughters are too big for him now but she doesn't want to sell him because she's had him since he was a foal—"

"Whoa, information overload!" said Jess with a smile.

"Anyway, I *did* ride Pepper!" Milly went on. "Emily and I went for a ride in the woods together. It was so cool! Chris asked me if I'd like to ride him again tomorrow. I had to say no 'cause we're doing genie stuff but I really hope she asks me another time. . . ."

"I'm sure she will," Jess said.

"It's been funny having a day without magic," Milly went on.

Jess nodded. "Yeah." She felt almost guilty when she realized she'd actually enjoyed it. She'd imagined that training to be a genie was going to be great fun, but after all the things that had happened she was beginning to wonder.

Magic seems to bring us nothing but trouble, she reflected with a sigh.

"I can't wait to get started on the genie book again tomorrow," Milly burbled on as she started to get changed. "Mr. Foxtrot's horrible. I bet we trick him really brilliantly. This is going to be fun!"

Jess chewed the end of her pen anxiously. She really hoped Milly was right.

As the sun rose the next morning, Jess, Michael, Jason, and Milly hurried to Sheerstock Avenue, where Arthur Foxtrot lived.

His house, number eleven, had a blue front door with a polished brass handle. In front of the house was a small, neat garden—a square of grass surrounded by three regimented rows of purple, yellow, and white pansies.

"Okay, here goes," Jess said, taking the lamp out of her bag.

"Ready to get tricking, Jase?" asked Michael, his dark hair sticking up wildly.

Jason nodded. "I think so." He had a few ideas but it all depended on what Mr. Foxtrot was going to wish for—and he knew he wouldn't have long before he had to grant the wish one way or another.

"Hang on," said Michael. "I've just thought of something! When Foxtrot rubs the lamp, Jase will be in his power like I was in Ollie's—so how will we get Foxtrot to say the 'Genie be free' bit?"

Jason stared at him. "I hadn't thought of that!"

There was a moment's silence.

"I've got an idea," said Jess slowly. "Get into the lamp, Jason."

Jason took a deep breath. "Genie me!" he whispered, and vanished down the spout.

Milly and Michael watched expectantly as Jess rubbed the well-worn brass. Jason whooshed back out in genie form.

"Now I'm the wish-maker," Jess declared. "And my wish is that you go back inside the lamp and grant a *single* wish for Mr. Arthur Foxtrot! Then you will be back under my control."

Jason grinned. "Your wish is my command!" He shrank and spiraled back up the brass spout.

"Impressive, Jess," said Michael, his bleary eyes full of admiration. "I mean—it's not even six thirty in the morning! That's totally devious!"

"I think 'in-genie-ous' is the word you're looking for!" Jess replied with a grin.

She and Michael watched from the wall as Milly placed the lamp on the front doorstep, rang the brass doorbell, and then turned and raced back down the drive. Michael and Jess ran away too. They all hid behind a parked car farther down the street.

"The door's opening," Jess hissed.

"This is the big one," said Michael nervously. "If Jase messes this up, we can forget about being genies, going back to London—all of it!"

Inside the lamp, Jason heard the click of the front door—quickly followed by Mr. Foxtrot's gruff voice. "Yes? Who's there?"

Suddenly the lamp was kicked. It fell sideways with a loud clatter and Jason cannoned into the wall. "Ow!" he muttered. Then he tensed in excitement as he felt the lamp being lifted up into the air. This could be it! The moment that he became a genie ready to grant Mr. Foxtrot's wish. But not just any genie—a genie who was up for playing tricks.

Rub the lamp, he willed Foxtrot. *Go on, rub it!*

"What on earth is this doing here?" Mr. Foxtrot muttered. "Dusty old thing."

The next second, Jason felt a familiar warm swirling sensation, as if the lamp was being polished.

Whoosh!

Jason only just had time to picture his genie disguise before he shot out of the lamp and landed in the garden directly in front of Mr. Foxtrot.

"What the . . . !" Mr. Foxtrot exclaimed. He dropped the lamp and staggered back.

Jason quickly checked to make sure the street was still deserted, then folded his arms. "I am a genie," he boomed in his loud mystical voice, enjoying the look of utter shock on Mr. Foxtrot's snooty face. "Your wish is my command!"

"But . . . but . . ." Mr. Foxtrot was turning paler by the moment.

Jason uncrossed his arms. "I am a genie," he repeated, lowering his voice. "I can grant a wish for you if you'd like. What *is* your wish?"

Suddenly, Mr. Foxtrot's face cleared. "Ahh . . . Of course! This is a *dream*," he said in a jovial tone. "Well, now, Genie, if you *are* here to grant my wish, then I'd better be quick before I wake up, hadn't I?" A crafty look spread over his face. "All right, here it is. I wish that *I* could answer every question at the Trivia Team Challenge today. Every single one!"

Jason's thoughts raced. So, *that* was the wish—now how could he twist it? An idea sprang into his mind, and he clapped his hands together. . . .

"Your wish is granted!" he exclaimed, grinning as he imagined the way the wish would turn out. "Now, put the lamp down, go back inside, and go to bed!"

"Go to bed?" Mr. Foxtrot frowned. "I must say, I'm not entirely convinced I'm even asleep. This is the most remarkably real dream I've ever had."

"Maybe so," said Jason with a sly smile. "But if it *wasn't* a dream, how else could I do *this*?"

And in a blast of green smoke, he swooshed back into the lamp.

Mr. Foxtrot cried out and dropped the lamp with a clatter. "Note to self," he muttered. "No more strong cheese late at night. Not ever." Then he swayed back inside and shut the door with a bang.

Milly, Jess, and Michael burst out from their hiding place and swapped elated looks as they hurried toward Mr. Foxtrot's doorstep.

Jess snatched up the lamp. "Genie be free!" she whispered.

The next second, Jason was standing there, grinning, dressed in his normal clothes again.

"Good work, mate!" Michael slapped him on the back as he steered him down the drive.

"Are you okay, Jase?" Milly asked.

"Yeah, I'm fine." Jason's eyes gleamed mischievously. "But Mr. Foxtrot's not going to be!"

"Why?" Jess demanded.

"Yeah, how did you twist his wish?" Michael asked.

"Aha!" Jason tapped his nose. "Not telling. You can all just wait and see!"

And no matter how much they badgered him on the way home, he wouldn't say a single word more.

When they got back, they sneaked in through the back door. The house was still quiet.

"Doesn't sound like Mum and Mark are up yet," Jess said quietly. "Let's go and tell Skribble how we've got on."

"I guess we may as well," Michael agreed. "Seeing as Jason won't talk to us, maybe the worm will!"

"Skribble never did say he was sorry after snapping at me," said Milly sadly. "And last night he didn't come out when I tried to say good night."

"Let's see if our news makes him less grumpy," Jess

suggested, leading the way upstairs and into the girls' bedroom.

"All right, Worm, you talking to us today?" Michael pulled out the book from Milly's pink pillowcase. "It's bright and early, and we've been sorting stuff for Step Five."

"So far so good," said Jason brightly as Michael started turning through the pages. "I hope!"

They waited for the usual muffled moans or a barrage of abuse. But the book stayed silent. Michael flicked through to the back cover without finding Skribble, and started flicking backward through the pages again.

"Come on, Skribble," said Jess, "where are you hiding?"

"He's not here," Michael announced, reaching the front of the book.

"Don't muck around," said Jason. "He's *got* to be."

"Well, he's not." Michael was turning the pages more urgently now. "See? No worm."

Jess snatched the handbook off him and shook it upside down. "Skribble, where are you?"

Nothing.

"He's gone," whispered Milly. "He's really *gone*!"

Chapter Twenty-four

The four children stared at the empty book. Suddenly Michael hit his forehead. "What are we doing? We're being stupid. We can easily find him!"

"We can?" Jess said in surprise.

"Of course! We've got our own guaranteed Skribble detector, you dummies—right here!" Michael held up the lamp. "We'll just *wish* to find him!"

"I'll be genie." Jess grabbed the lamp. "Genie me!"

She whooshed away and quickly pictured herself in her glam-chic genie outfit as Milly rubbed the lamp and summoned her back into the human world.

"I wish that Skribble was here right now," declared Milly.

Glittery outfit and tiara perfectly in place, Jess tried bringing her hands together—but they just made an ordinary, quiet clap. "Nothing's happening," she said in confusion.

"I'll try again," said Milly. "I wish that we could find

Skribble . . . um, please?"

But Jess just stood there. "It's no good!" she said.

Jason gasped. "Maybe the lamp's broken?"

"Quick, Mil," said Michael, "wish for something else."

"I wish . . ." Milly shrugged. "I wish I had a chocolate banana in my right hand!"

Jess clapped. "From dust I conjure it!"

And as the last booming word left her mouth, a chocolate banana duly appeared in Milly's hand.

"The magic *must* be working!" Michael took the banana and bit into it moodily. "So why can't we use it to find Skribble?"

"I don't know. Guess we'll just have to use our eyes instead," said Jess. "He's so small, he can't have gone far. Milly, you and I can search up here. Michael, you and Jason look down in the den. He might have crawled out when we were last there."

"Poor Skribble," murmured Milly, tears welling in her eyes. "I should have looked for him sooner! If anything's happened to him—"

"Don't think that way, sis," said Michael softly. "We'll find him. Operation Worm Hunt has begun!"

By eleven o'clock that morning, after hours of frantic rummaging all about the house, the search parties regrouped on the landing.

"We've looked everywhere," said Michael. Scowling, he kicked one of Milly's big furry rabbit slippers back into her bedroom. "Nothing."

Just then, Mark bounded up the stairs. "Hi, guys. Sorry to interrupt your game, but Jason, can I borrow you for some last-minute studying?"

"It's *not* a game," cried Milly in frustration. "It's real, and nobody knows and it's just not fair!" She flew into the bedroom and slammed the door shut.

Mark frowned and looked at Michael. "Everything all right?"

"Fine," said Jason, forcing a bright smile. "And of course I'll help. How are you feeling—confident?"

"Nervous!" Mark admitted, ushering Jason down the stairs. "But those 'improve your memory' techniques you taught me have really helped—I'm trying to think of each fact as a landmark on a journey that I take in my head. Thing is, it's a really bizarre journey. . . ."

"Tell us about it." Jess sighed as her stepdad and brother moved out of earshot.

Suddenly there was a short, sharp shriek from Milly in the bedroom. Jess and Michael stared at each other for a split second and then raced to the door. But before they could reach it, Milly threw it open, looking wide-eyed.

"What's happened?" Michael demanded.

"I've found him," whispered Milly. "He must have been hiding in my slipper and when you kicked it, he fell out. But . . . but . . ."

She pointed wordlessly into the room. Michael and Jess ran inside.

There was the big, furry rabbit slipper, lying upside down. And there was Skribble on the floor beside it.

The bookworm had turned as gray as clay. His little eyes were shut, and his body was lying completely still.

Michael crouched down and held a finger in front of Skribble's tiny line of a mouth.

"Oh, no . . ." Jess swallowed hard. "Has he . . . is he . . . ?"

"It's okay. He's still alive." Michael scooped Skribble up in both hands. "I caught the tiniest breath on my finger when I held it in front of his mouth."

"He looks really sick," Milly fretted, stroking the bookworm gently. "Oh, Skribble! Poor, lovely, clever Skribble, we've been so worried about you!"

Skribble's little eyes blinked open. "Milly?" he gasped feebly. "Is that you?"

"I'm here." Milly looked around at Jess. "His skin's so cold! Feel it!"

"We need to keep him warm and comfortable," said

Jess. "Let's put him back in the book."

"No!" Skribble gasped. "No, please!"

Jess, Michael, and Milly exchanged confused looks.

"Not the book!" Skribble croaked. "No!"

"Okay. Try to take it easy. . . ." Milly hated to see him so distressed. She dived down and scrabbled about under her bed, coming back with a thick scrunchie for tying back her hair. She laid the little fabric ring on her pillow. "Put him down there instead, Michael."

Michael did so. Skribble wrapped his little body around the soft scrunchie and clung there.

"What's good for a shock?" Michael wondered. "I know! Jess, your mum's got some cooking sherry in the kitchen!"

Jess gave him a stern look. "He needs a hot, sweet cup of tea."

"I'll go and get some!" Milly declared. She fled out of the room.

Jess looked at Skribble, lying so still and quiet. "It seems so long since he first turned up," she said in a hushed voice. "It's hard to believe it's been barely a week."

"Dumb worm gets under your skin." Michael sighed. "Doesn't look too clever now, does he?"

Skribble opened one eye. "I am still *extremely* clever," he said faintly, "thank you very much."

Jess half smiled. "Oh, Skribble, we've been so worried about you. We tried to find you using magic, but it didn't work."

Skribble blinked weakly. "Magic cannot affect other magical beings while they are in the human world. It is one of the oldest genie laws, to stop rival genies from harming one another."

Michael raised an eyebrow. "Did that used to happen, then?"

"Oh, yes." Skribble's eyelids flickered shut. "Genies very rarely see eye to eye. And disputes could swiftly get out of hand. So, ages past, a law was decreed that any dispute must be settled properly in the Genie Realm. . . ."

Milly came back—a mug of tea in one hand and a dusty bottle of cooking sherry in the other. Putting the drinks on the floor, she produced a teaspoon from her pocket and held out a little of the tea. Skribble opened his eyes, sniffed it, then turned his head away.

"Try mixing it with the cooking sherry," suggested Michael. He opened the bottle and poured a drop onto the spoon. This time, Skribble drank a little, and licked his tiny lips.

"Maybe we *should* put him back in the book," Jess suggested.

"No!" Skribble said hoarsely. "The book has turned

against me. It has thrown me out."

"Was it because you ate that whole page?" Milly asked.

"Yes." Skribble nodded. "And not just any old page . . . A page awash with active magic . . . new words and pictures being brought into being." He angled his head toward the teaspoon, and Milly let him drink a little more. "The magic I ate was too much for this small, puny body to cope with." Skribble hiccuped. "The book could have helped me if it chose, but it didn't. . . . Oh, if only I could change back . . ."

Jess frowned. "Change back? What do you mean?"

The bookworm ignored her. "You must complete the next step quickly," he whispered. "It is very important."

"But *why* is it so important?" Jess asked. "Skribble, I don't understand. Why do you want us to become genies so badly?"

But Skribble's eyes had closed once more.

Milly looked at the handbook. "Please, Book," she said, stroking its cover. "Please help us to help Skribble. You've been together such a long time . . . maybe too long for him to live without you. I expect you thought you had to teach Skribble a lesson—but please, won't you help him now? Otherwise, he might . . . well . . ."

The book shook a little; then its cover swung open. Milly

gasped and pulled her hand back. The front page started slowly to turn. As Michael, Jess, and Milly watched, a narrow strip of paper started to tear itself away from the top edge, curling over like a wood shaving until it fluttered free of the book and fell to the duvet.

Then the book snapped shut again.

Cautiously, Milly picked up the yellowed curl of paper and stretched it between her fingers. "It's a blanket!" she breathed. "The book's given us a bookworm's blanket!"

"Let's wrap him up in it, then," said Jess.

Milly sat down on the bed beside Skribble and tenderly covered him with the curl of paper. Skribble crept down inside it and took a deep, trembling breath. Milly stroked the back of his neck with one finger. "There, now, Skribble. You'll be all right," she whispered.

After a few moments, Jess frowned. "Is it my imagination, or is he starting to look a little more like his old self?"

"I think he is." Milly gasped. "Look, the paper's changing!"

Jess saw that she was right. The yellow curl was darkening to a deep brown, and Skribble was growing pinker. "It must be drawing out all that active magic he ate," she realized.

"He's going to get better," said Milly with delight. "I

just know he is! Come on. We should leave him alone now to rest properly."

Jess screwed the top back on the cooking sherry. "I'll put this back before anyone realizes it's gone."

"And I'll get Jason away from Dad and tell him the good news," said Michael. "See you guys down there."

Once Jess and Michael had gone, Milly couldn't resist one last peep at Skribble. "Why did you choose to hide in my slipper?" she whispered, crouching beside the bed.

"Because it was soft and warm," said Skribble sleepily. "And because it was yours."

Milly smiled and pulled the duvet over him, feeling warm and tingly from top to toe. She heard the worm mumbling in his sleep: "I'm sorry, so very sorry, your worships. . . . I'll change for the better! Truly I will . . ."

She felt funny eavesdropping, so she turned to go. But then she noticed the book was lying open again, back at the end of Step Four. One phrase leaped out at her:

Unworthy are they who would seek to use the spirit and strife of others to achieve their own ends!

Milly frowned and closed the book again. Then, a little uneasily, she hurried from the room.

Chapter Twenty-five

When the children arrived at the town hall for the big trivia challenge that afternoon, they found it was packed with people. Jess, Michael, Jason, and Milly made their way through the crowds and slipped into a row of seats near the front of the hall. Before them was a stage with a central microphone. On either side of it were two long tables, each with four chairs and four buzzers, where the teams would sit and compete. A banner across the stage read, GRAND TRIVIA TEAM CHALLENGE IN AID OF GUIDE DOGS FOR THE BLIND. The eight teams taking part sat in the waiting area just in front of the stage.

"This whole thing is lame to the max," grumbled Michael. "I think Skribble had the right idea, taking a sick day."

"He's not pretending," said Milly defensively. They had left the bookworm safely recovering under her duvet. "Anyway, don't you want to see Mr. Foxtrot get tricked?"

"*If* I've granted the wish properly," Jason fretted. It

seemed a long time since Mr. Foxtrot had made the wish that morning. Would his trick work?

Jess half smiled. "You sound as nervous as Mark looks!"

Mark was white-faced and clearly worried. Beside him was a woman in her fifties with long gray hair and large glasses, and a tall dark-haired man who looked to be around Mark's age.

Ginny and David, Jason thought. Mark had told him all about the other team members—Ginny worked in the town's newsdealer and was good at questions on TV, film, and books, while David was an accountant and knew all about sports.

Mr. Foxtrot was pacing around the table. "Concentration," he announced, pointing at Ginny. "Focus," he said to David. Then he looked at Mark and sighed. "Oh, for heaven's sake, just get the answers right!"

Ann, who was standing behind Mark, looked about to say something, but Mark squeezed her arm and shook his head.

The quizmaster, Mr. Evans, walked onto the stage with a microphone. "Well, I think we're just about ready to start!" he announced. "So, let's have a bit of hush!"

People stopped talking and began to make their way to their seats. Ann kissed Mark on the head and looked for a free place to sit. The kids had "accidentally" forgotten to save her a chair, so she sat a couple of rows behind them.

"Welcome to Moreways Meet's sixth Grand Trivia Team Challenge," Mr. Evans said. "It's great to see so many of you here today turning out to support such a worthwhile cause. The challenge will commence shortly and will be followed by a break for refreshments and then a tea dance. . . ."

"What is a tea dance, anyway?" Milly whispered.

"Old people dancing and having tea," Jess said. "I asked Mum."

"Ultralame!" Michael cringed. "Soon as the challenge is over we're out of here. . . ."

Mr. Evans picked up a folder. "And so, on to the quiz. The teams will take turns to compete in pairs, answering questions in six categories—geography, sports, science and math, entertainment, current affairs, and finally history. The winning team of each pair will go through to the semifinals and then the two winners of the semifinals will go head-to-head in the grand finale. May I ask the first two teams to join me, please: the Foxtrot Four and the East Street Eagles."

The audience broke out into polite applause. "Go on, Dad!" Milly whispered as Mark's team made their way from the waiting area onto the stage. They took their places to the left of Mr. Evans, while the East Street Eagles sat on the right. Milly saw that the team captain was Barry, the owner of Junk and Disorderly.

"Fingers on the buzzers, please, teams, and here we go." Mr. Evans read out the first question. "In which mountain range is Mount Everest?"

The Himalayas, Jason thought instantly. He had asked Mark the same question only that morning. Mark buzzed, but Barry beat him to it. However, before Barry could say the answer, Mr. Foxtrot jumped up.

"The Alps!" he shouted.

There were a few startled gasps from the audience and everyone stared at him.

Mr. Evans blinked. "Please, Arthur, sit down. You must know the rules better than anyone—no speaking out unless you buzz and I call your name."

Mr. Foxtrot's face turned crimson. "Sorry, sorry," he blustered, hastily sitting down. "Don't know what came over me. . . ."

Jess, Michael, and Milly turned to look at Jason. He grinned but didn't say anything.

Mr. Evans cleared his throat. "Let's start again with another question—which American state is nicknamed 'the Sunshine State'?"

Again Mark buzzed but before Mr. Evans could ask him

for the answer, Mr. Foxtrot was on his feet. "Florida!" he yelled.

This time there was a hum of noise as people on the other quiz teams and members of the audience turned to each other and began whispering.

"What is he doing?" Jess hissed. "I mean, at least he got the answer right this time but . . ." She looked pointedly at Jason. "What's going on?"

But Jason only smiled.

"Will you *please* sit down, Arthur!" Mr. Evans said sharply. "I cannot accept your answer if you do not buzz. It's the rules!" He turned to the chattering audience. "May I have some hush, please?"

"Yes!" boomed Foxtrot.

There was still more excited whispering. Foxtrot had turned as red as a sunburned beetroot as he sat back in his chair. Mark swapped bemused looks with David and Ginny.

Michael elbowed Jason. "'Fess up. What's going on with Foxtrot?"

"Well . . ." Jason decided to put them out of their misery. "He wished that he could answer *every single question* at the quiz this afternoon. And so that's the wish I granted."

A slow smile spread over Michael's face. "You mean

he's going to answer *anything* that *anyone* is asked?"

Jason nodded.

"Even if he doesn't know the right answer?" said Jess wonderingly.

"Yep." Jason grinned. "Guess he should have told me he wanted to answer them all correctly, shouldn't he?"

"Oh, Jase!" Michael said, punching his arm. "That's priceless!"

Milly chuckled. "Good one, Jase!"

"And for the third time," Mr. Evans announced. "The first geography question of the round . . ." He glanced warily at Foxtrot. "In which ocean is the island of Mauritius?"

Foxtrot half leaped up from his chair. Grabbing the seat of it with both hands, he pulled himself back down, his lips tightly shut. But the magic impelling him to answer was too great. "The Pacific!" he roared.

This time the buzz of chatter in the audience was loud enough to fill the room. It was clear no one had ever behaved like this before.

Mr. Evans stomped furiously to the front of the stage. "This is your final warning, Arthur! You're spoiling it for everyone. One more word and you're disqualified—do you understand?"

"Of course!" Foxtrot cried.

Mark grabbed his arm and pulled him down into his

seat. Ginny and David rounded on him. Jason couldn't hear what they were saying, but it was clear from the looks on their faces that they were not happy at all.

Mr. Evans looked very red and cross as he returned to his chair. "Which country does Portugal border?"

"France!" bellowed Foxtrot, jumping to his feet before anyone had a chance to buzz. "No, Spain! Or is it Germany?"

"That's it!" Mr. Evans yelled. He pointed to the door. "You're out!"

Foxtrot squeaked like a mouse caught in a trap. "No! You can't do this! Not to *me*!"

Barry stood up crossly. "You think you're better than anyone else, don't you, Foxtrot?"

"Of course I do, and with very good reason!" Foxtrot cried—then slapped both hands over his mouth with a horrified look, as if trying to stop any more words from escaping. "Tell me I didn't just say that!"

"You're disqualified, Arthur," said Mr. Evans. He signaled to two of the ushers who'd been helping people to their seats, and they headed quickly for the stage.

"Could you come this way, sir?" one of them asked.

"Yes!" Foxtrot snapped. "I mean—no! Please, let me stay!" He looked around wildly. "I want to win. I *deserve* to win! I've GOT to win!"

"This way, please, sir," the other usher said, taking him by his arm.

Mr. Foxtrot was led out down the stairs at the side of the stage, arguing furiously. "This is preposterous! This is ridiculous. . . ." He tried to pull away from the ushers but was firmly propelled toward the door.

"Poor man," a woman in front of the Worthingtons said to her companion. "It must be the strain."

Her companion sighed. "Old Arthur always was a silly beggar."

Michael leaned over Milly and high-fived with Jason. "Way to go, Jase!"

"That was a great trick!" Milly agreed. "I bet we'll have passed Step Five easily!"

"The only trouble is," Jess said slowly, "Mark's team is now a member short. If that means they lose . . ."

Jason pulled a face. "Oh, no, I hadn't thought of that! The book said that no one else must suffer because of the wish." He gulped. "And now Mark and his team are a man down."

Michael slapped a hand to his forehead. "You know what that means, don't you—if they *do* lose, we're going to have failed the step after all!"

Chapter Twenty-six

" **I** f we've failed this step, that's it for the genie training!" said Jess anxiously. "No second chances, remember?"

"Look, it *might* be okay," said Jason hopefully. "I've been helping Mark with his fact learning and he's loads better now. The team might not need Mr. Foxtrot if Mark can answer all his questions correctly."

"I hope you're right, Jase," Michael said as the hall door was shut firmly after Foxtrot and the Trivia Team Challenge resumed.

Mr. Evans cleared his throat. "Let's start again. Which is the longest river in Scotland?"

Mark buzzed first.

Mr. Evans nodded. "Foxtrot Four?"

"The Tay!"

"Correct." Mr. Evans looked very relieved to finally have the first question out of the way. "And the second geography question: Into which sea does the Nile flow?"

Mark and Barry both buzzed, but again Mark was just a fraction ahead.

"Foxtrot Four, again," said Mr. Evans.

"The Mediterranean."

"Correct," Mr. Evans said again. "That's two points for the Foxtrot Four."

The trivia challenge seemed to go on and on as all the different teams took their turns. But Mark did really well. In fact, all three remaining of the Foxtrot Four answered lots of questions. They won the first round by a whisker, and then won their semifinal by several points.

"They don't need Foxtrot at all!" said Jess as Mark, David, and Ginny went back onto the stage for the final against a team of glamorous middle-aged women called the Brooke Close Babes.

"If Dad's team wins then there's no way that the book can say you've made anyone else suffer!" Milly said excitedly to Jason. "It'll *have* to pass us!"

"Go, Dad! Go, Dad!" Michael chanted under his breath.

It was very close, with the two teams neck and neck until a final tiebreaking question:

"Is it possible for a man in Wales to marry his widow's sister?" Mr. Evans asked them.

Jason's heart leaped, and Mark's finger was on the buzzer instantly.

Mr. Evans turned to him in a moment. "Foxtrot Four?"

"No, it's not possible!" Mark exclaimed, with a look toward Jason in the crowd. "If a man's got a widow, he's dead—he can't marry anyone!"

"Correct!" Mr. Evans declared. "The Foxtrot Four—er, *Three*—are the winners!"

"Yes!" Michael jumped up and punched the air as the audience burst into applause. Jess whooped. Milly flung her arms around Jason, and Ann hurried from her seat to join in the hug. Jess and Michael hastily drew away in case she tried to hug them too.

Up on the stage, Mark looked like he could hardly believe it as Ginny hugged him and David pumped his hand. The other teams came over and congratulated them too.

Mr. Evans produced a silver trophy from behind his podium. "Would the winners kindly come up and receive their prize?" he announced, sparking a fresh round of applause. The kids all cheered as Mark, David, and Ginny collected their trophy.

David held the trophy above his head in victory. "Thank you very much!" he said.

"I suppose the name Foxtrot Four doesn't really fit anymore," Mr. Evans commented. "How about . . . the Foxtrotless Three?"

Ginny grinned. "I think the name on the trophy should be Worthington's Wonders!" She pushed Mark forward. "Seeing as this man here, Mark Worthington, was the real star of the team!"

Mark looked pleased but embarrassed. "Well, we *all* answered questions."

"But you got so many right!" said David. "Must come from owning your own bookshop!"

"Would you like to say a few words, Mark?" Mr. Evans said, handing him the microphone.

Mark nodded. "I'd just like to say a huge thank-you to one person in particular—my nine-year-old stepson, Jason. Without his help preparing me for this quiz, I wouldn't be here!"

Jason went bright red as Michael hauled him to his feet.

"Here he is!" Michael shouted.

Mark motioned to Jason. "Come up here!"

Milly nudged him along the row, and Jason stumbled to the front in a daze. The audience clapped again as he went up the steps onto the stage.

"What a nail-biting event they've all given us," said Mr. Evans. "I give you—Worthington's Wonders!"

Everyone left the stage to the sound of cheering. Mark and Jason went to join Ann, Jess, Michael, and Milly. "Well done!" Ann said, kissing Mark. "You were brilliant!"

Milly hugged him. "You got so many questions right, Dad!"

"Thanks to Jason," Mark said. "I could never have answered all those questions without your help, mate."

"No problem," Jason said, glad to be surrounded by his family looking so happy.

A young, slim woman with blond corkscrew curls came over, holding a notebook and a tape recorder. "Hi," she said, looking at Mark. "I don't mean to intrude, but I'm a journalist for the local paper. My name's Sarah Sellick." She raised her eyebrows. "Sounds like your team had some excitement today even before your victory! I bumped into Arthur Foxtrot outside the hall and had a little chat."

"Did he answer your questions?" asked Jason innocently.

Sarah nodded. "Even the ones I was asking other people! I couldn't shut him up! Anyway, I'd love to get a few words from you—and from this young man here." Sarah smiled at Jason. "Is it true you helped your dad prepare?"

"He's not really my . . ." Jason stopped, his eyes meeting Mark's. "Yeah. It's true."

"Great! Let's pop nearer to the stage, where it's a bit quieter," Sarah suggested.

"Think I'll come too," Michael announced. "You might

want to quote me; I'm Jason's older stepbrother—taught him everything he knows. . . ."

Jason play-shoved Michael. "As if!"

Milly and Jess watched as Jason, Michael, and Mark set off with Sarah Sellick.

"Cokes all around, girls?" asked Ann.

Jess and Milly nodded. They all picked a slow path through the thronging people toward the bar at the side of the busy room.

"Hey, Jess! Over here!"

Jess looked around and, to her surprise, spotted Colette pushing her way through the crowd toward her.

"I've been looking for you," said Colette, reaching her at last. "I thought I'd stop by to see how your dad had got on."

"His team won!" Jess said, delighted that Colette had bothered to come. "I can hardly believe it! He's being interviewed by some journalist right now."

"By the way," Colette went on, "did that weird couple find you okay?"

Jess frowned. "What weird couple?"

"This man and woman came up to me about five minutes ago, asked me if I knew you, and where you and your brothers and sister lived. I didn't tell them, of course," Colette added quickly, seeing Jess's shocked expression.

"They looked sort of . . . weird. Suntans and white teeth, and staring eyes . . ."

With a sick feeling, Jess realized she was describing the couple they'd seen at the junk shop, and again on the way back from Colette's house. "Where are they now?"

Colette's eyes skimmed across the crowd. "Can't see them. They must have gone." She looked at Jess. "You look pale. Is everything cool?"

Jess nodded. "Yeah. Fine." But her mind was racing. Why had the weird couple come here? Why did they want to know where she lived? "I—I'd better get back to Mum and everyone."

"I'd better get going, too," said Colette. "See you tomorrow!"

"Yeah, later," Jess replied.

As Colette fought her way back through the crowd, Jess's skin was prickling. *Stay calm,* she thought. *Just find the others—now!*

She glanced to the front of the hall. Sarah Sellick was still interviewing Mark and Jason. Michael was leaning backward on his chair, trying to catch Sarah's eye. Jess waved to him urgently.

Seeing the panicked expression on her face, Michael came over. "What's up?"

"You know that man and woman we saw the other day

at the top of Colette's road?" Jess shuddered. "Well, they were here in the hall. They saw Colette and asked her if she knew me. They wanted to know where we lived!"

"Seriously?" Michael ran a hand through his hair. "That's a bit weird. Why would they want to know that?"

"I don't know. They looked at me and Milly so strangely in the junk shop. The lamp was wrapped up, but they kept staring, as if they were trying to see what it was. . . ."

"And then they turn up a few days later when we're all around together," said Michael. "And now they want to know who we are and where we live."

"They're after us," Jess said simply. She looked at Michael. "And . . . I think they're *magic*!"

To her relief, Michael didn't laugh. He thought for a second and then nodded. "We should talk to the others about this."

"Quick as we can," Jess agreed, relieved. Having Michael take her side made her feel a bit better.

"Hey, you two—over here!" Hearing Ann's voice, they turned. The interview had finished and Ann, Mark, Jason, and Milly were all standing by the door.

"Coming!" Jess called.

"What were you two talking about?" Mark asked curiously as they walked over. "You looked deep in conversation."

"Just talking about which would be worse," Michael said lightly. "Going to a tea dance or having your nose hairs pulled out by a killer monkey with dirty fingernails."

Mark grinned. "The tea dance, obviously!"

As they left the hall, Milly and Jason fell into step beside Jess. "What were you and Michael really talking about?" Milly whispered curiously. "Was it genie stuff?"

Jess glanced at their parents. "Later."

"Is something wrong?" said Jason, frowning.

Jess hesitated. She wanted to say no, so that he and Milly didn't worry.

But her every instinct was screaming that something was very wrong indeed. . . .

Chapter Twenty-seven

The kids headed upstairs as soon as they got home, while their parents cracked open a bottle of wine in the kitchen to toast the Worthington's Wonders' victory.

Jess and Milly led the way into their bedroom. Milly ran to check on Skribble. He was still asleep by her pillow, looking loads better.

Michael shut the door and leaned against it.

"Okay, what's going on?" Jason demanded.

Jess put the book down on the bed. "It's that man and woman we saw, with the freaky eyes. They came to the town hall—asking where we live!" She repeated what Colette had told her.

"But why would they be asking about us?" said Jason, alarmed. "What have we done?"

"Magic," said Michael simply.

Milly gasped. "Maybe they're evil genies! Skribble said that genies used to try to hurt each other. . . . Maybe they want to get *us*!"

"Don't be silly. They couldn't be evil genies. . . ." Jess faltered, glancing at Michael. "Could they?"

Michael didn't answer.

"I bet they are!" Milly exclaimed. "What are we going to do? They might use magic on us. They might turn us all into frogs or something!"

"Maybe they're just normal people," said Jason reasonably, "who happened to be asking where we lived. Maybe it's something to do with the launch of the bookshop?"

Suddenly, the book began to shake. Its cover flipped open and the pages started to turn.

The noise woke Skribble. He raised his head from the hair scrunchie. "So you're back," he said sleepily. "Were you successful? Hmmm?"

But no one answered. They were staring at the book. Two new pictures had appeared. The first showed Mr. Foxtrot picking up the lamp that morning.

A most excellent entrapment, read the caption. *A deception cleverly achieved.*

But it was the picture underneath that was holding everyone's attention. It showed them seated in the trivia challenge audience, laughing and joking.

And there, a few rows behind them, sat the mysterious man and woman. They were watching the children intently with their dark, glittering eyes.

A single sentence was written beneath the picture.

"'Beware of those who watch you,'" Jason read slowly. He stared around. "That was what the book said before. In that picture of us in London with the shadows behind us . . ."

"It's them!" Milly gasped. "They've been watching us all along!"

"Stalking us, more like!" breathed Michael. He started flicking back through the book, stopping at the picture of Colette outside her house at the end of Step Four.

Jess froze. "Oh, no . . ."

Standing by the wall, watching Colette, the couple was clearly visible.

"They weren't in that picture before," said Jason, chewing his lip. "Were they?"

"I'm sure they weren't." Michael turned back to the end of Step Three, to the picture of Jess in the park. A cold chill shivered through him. There was no shadow on the grass now.

Instead, the dark-haired woman was crouched down just behind Jess, her eyes picked out in the deepest, blackest ink.

"She's close enough to touch," breathed Jess. She turned away, covering her face with her hands.

Michael put the book down on the bed, his heart banging

with fear. "How come the book didn't show us before?"

"Maybe it's the book's way of telling us they're closer now," said Jason. "Closer than ever."

"I don't like this," Milly said, sounding frightened. "Michael, I don't like this at all."

"What are you all babbling about?" Skribble asked tetchily. "Disturbing my rest like this, dear, oh, dear . . ." Pulling himself off the scrunchie, he crawled toward the book. He inched onto the page with the picture and stopped dead.

"No!" The word was barely more than an intake of breath. "No, no, no!" Skribble began to back away, his face terrified.

"Skribble, what is it?" Jess said in alarm.

"They've come for me!" Skribble moaned. "They're here to take me back!" With a frightened howl, he dived into a hole in the book. The pages rattled as if he was shivering deep inside.

Michael, Milly, Jess, and Jason stared at each other, frightened and unsure.

"Skribble!" said Milly desperately. "Please come out! Talk to us!"

"Uh-oh," said Jason. He could hear footsteps outside. "Someone's coming!"

"Who?" Jess and Michael gasped in unison.

The door handle turned sharply.

Michael threw the book in the air in alarm, and Jess caught it neatly and slid it beneath her pillow—just as Ann came looking around the door.

"Come on, you antisocial lot!" she said brightly. "Join the celebration downstairs." They could hear music floating up from the living room. "But first, tell me . . . Will you all come and help us set things up for the party in the shop tomorrow before we open?"

"Uh . . ." Jess forced herself to nod and smile. "Yeah! Sure!"

"Thank you!" Ann grinned. "In that case, Mark and I will let you come with us to the Chinese restaurant tonight for a celebration meal!"

"Oh . . . great!" said Michael. He felt like hiding under the bed, not going out for food—and from the looks on the others' faces he suspected they felt the same.

Milly looked seriously at Michael. "Maybe we should tell Ann and Dad. . . ."

"Tell me what?" said Ann, puzzled.

"Er, how excited we are about the opening party," said Michael. "And dinner! Great. We'll be down in a minute."

"Good!" said Ann, practically bouncing out of the

room. "We'll be off in half an hour."

As soon as the door closed, Michael scowled at Milly. "We made a vow, sis, remember? No telling *anyone* about magic!"

"But things are getting really scary," said Milly, hugging herself.

Jess slipped an arm around her. "I know. I'm scared too. But if this couple is magic, what can Mum and Mark do?"

Jason sighed. "That's if they even believed us."

"We could show them the book!" Milly argued.

But the book suddenly shook with a noise like the rattle of a snake. An unmistakable warning sound that sent a shiver through them all.

"Maybe not, then," said Michael quickly.

"It's not fair." Milly's face crumpled. "We were doing so well. The magic was all so amazing, so much fun. . . ."

"Not anymore," muttered Jess. She jumped as the pages of the book fluttered open. One of the yellowing pages was glowing gold.

"It's the introduction to Step Six!" Michael realized. "And I can read it!"

"Then we passed Step Five," said Jason, rushing to see.

"I almost wish we hadn't," muttered Jess.

"Wait! Something must be wrong." Milly stared at the words on the page. "Just what are we meant to make of *that*?"

The Genie Handbook

The Sixth Step:
Great Revelations

Sometimes it is safer to do nothing.

Chapter Twenty-eight

Jess lay awake that night, thinking about the book's mysterious remark. *Sometimes it is safer to do nothing.* The words ran around her head.

Her stomach growled; she and the others had barely touched their food at the restaurant. And when sleep came, it was only fitfully. The genie lamp stood on her bedside table, gleaming dully in the glow from her alarm clock's luminous hands. As the clock clicked away the slow minutes, outside the window all was in blackness. Jess thought longingly of her old bedroom back in London, with its view of the well-lit, busy road.

If we'd never left London, none of this would have happened, she thought. *We wouldn't have gotten involved in magic and we wouldn't have weird people after us. Oh, I wish we were back there.*

The glowing hands of the clock were edging toward five-to-six in the morning when she heard Milly wake up.

"Jess?" Milly whispered.

"Yes?"

"I'm scared. I've just had a really bad dream."

"Come on," Jess said in a low voice, turning the light on and rubbing her eyes. "Let's get up." She got out of bed and threw Milly her robe and furry rabbit slippers. "We'll take the book down to the den and see if we can get Skribble to talk to us—tell us what he knows about the man and woman."

Milly got up. She warily took the book from under her pillow as if expecting it to bite her, and then they crept downstairs.

The door to the den was ajar.

"Why's it open?" Milly said nervously.

"I don't know," Jess whispered. Her heart in her throat, she nudged the door.

A ray of bright light immediately shone into her face. She opened her mouth to scream.

"It's all right; it's only us!" Michael's voice hissed from the staircase. "Jason came to find me. He couldn't sleep so we thought we'd come down here."

Jess's legs felt like jelly. She clutched the banister as she and Milly went down the stairs to join the boys. Michael and Jason were both carrying several flashlights. "Why didn't you switch the light on?" she demanded.

"Didn't want to draw attention to ourselves." Michael

padded around in his robe, switching on the flashlights he was holding to give them some light—a Spider-Man flashlight and that silly duck flashlight that Jason had gotten stuck in. . . .

"Why were you coming to the den?" Jason asked Milly.

"We couldn't sleep either," she replied. She held up the book. "We thought we could ask Skribble what he knows about the weird couple." She opened the book. "Skribble?"

Skribble's head popped out cautiously.

"Oh, Skribble," Milly said, feeling very relieved to see him. She carried the book over to the sofa and sat down. "Please will you tell us what's going on?"

"It's bad, isn't it?" said Michael anxiously.

"Yes." Skribble's little face was very grave. "I am afraid we may all be in great danger."

"Who are those people watching us?" Jason asked. "You know, the ones you saw in the book?"

Skribble sighed. "I believe they are genies."

"See!" Milly exclaimed, looking around at the others. "I *told* you they were evil genies!"

A cagey expression flitted across Skribble's face. "Yes," he said. "Yes. That's exactly what they are. Evil, wicked, and pernicious genies!"

"But what do they want with us, Skribble?" asked Michael. "Why did they want to know where we lived?"

"I fear it is my fault," Skribble said slowly. "It is time for you to know the truth about me. I am not merely a magical bookworm. You see, I . . . was once . . ." He looked down. "*I was once a great and powerful genie.*"

The children stared.

"You're kidding," said Michael.

"I most certainly am not!" Skribble said sharply. "I was a master of magic. But then, I found myself locked up! Imprisoned by miserable, petty-minded, pea-brained fools."

"Why?" asked Milly, her eyes wide. "What had you done?"

"Nothing," said Skribble sadly. "I had done nothing."

The book fluttered a little. Skribble gave the pages a wary look. "In any case," he went on hurriedly, "after I was locked away, I cleverly transformed myself into a bookworm and hid inside *The Genie Handbook* to escape their evil clutches. . . ."

"And then the library was ransacked, wasn't it?" Jason remembered. "The book was taken to the human world with you inside it. And you didn't have a lamp so there was no way back to your own land."

"Without a lamp, a genie is nothing," said Skribble

somberly. "Suffice to say, I became stuck in this form of a bookworm and dependent on the book's magic to sustain me."

"So *that's* what you meant about changing yourself back," Jess realized. "You wanted to change back into your real form—a genie."

"And you thought that if *we* became genies, we could do that for you," Milly said. "It all makes sense now. No wonder you wanted us to complete our training as soon as possible."

"But, Skribble, you told us magic doesn't work on other magical beings," Jason pointed out. "That's why we couldn't find you with magic when you vanished. So how could we have helped?"

"I had a plan." Skribble smiled sadly. "And very cunning it was, too. All I needed was a little more time . . . and your help."

"Oh, Skribble," said Milly. "I wish you'd told us sooner. You'll always have our help, whatever's the matter." She looked around at the others. "Won't he?"

Jess and Jason nodded.

Michael sighed. "I guess."

"Eh?" Skribble blinked. "Oh . . . Thank you . . ." He frowned, shook his head. "In any case, none of this is important! Not now that these two genies have arrived.

252

Their appearance here in the human world can only mean one thing—that they have come to take me back to the Genie Realm and punish me."

"Well, we won't let them!" Milly exclaimed.

"No way!" said Jason fiercely.

"Wait," said Skribble. "There is more."

"What sort of more?" said Michael suspiciously as the bookworm shifted uncomfortably on the page.

"These genies may be after *you* as well," Skribble admitted. "The magical books, although brought into the human world, were never meant to be *used* by humans. You may be punished for using genie magic."

Jess looked at him in horror. "*What?*"

"Punished by *genies!*" squeaked Jason.

"They'll use magic on us. . . ." Michael groaned. "Worm, d'you think maybe you could have told us that our training was against the law a bit sooner?"

Skribble hung his head.

"Let's not argue about it now," said Milly quickly. "What can we do, Skribble? Have you got a plan?"

"No," the bookworm admitted.

Michael huffed. "Well, things just get better and better."

"Wait a sec," said Jason. "We know genies can't use magic against other magical beings, right? Well, *we've* done magic—so how *can* they do anything to us?"

"Alas, you are still in training," Skribble reminded him. "Until you pass all six steps you are not *proper* magical beings."

"Which means they *can* use magic on us," Jess realized with a sinking heart.

Jason wasn't giving up. "But if they can use magic on us because we aren't *proper* genies . . . perhaps that means we can use magic back at *them*!"

"We couldn't find Skribble before," Michael reminded him.

"But that was before we passed Step Five," Jason argued. "Our magic's gotten stronger with every passing step, hasn't it?"

"It has indeed. . . ." Skribble looked thoughtful. "Yes, the four of you have shown great aptitude for the magical existence. Your powers have grown because you have worked together, planned together, and helped each other when things have gone wrong."

"*You've* helped us too, Skribble," said Milly loyally. "We're a team."

Michael nodded. "And there're five of us and only two of them." He forced an optimistic tone into his voice. "Together we can do it—we've got them outnumbered! What can they do to us?"

Suddenly the main lights snapped on, making them all jump.

There were two figures standing in the shadows at the top of the staircase.

Jess felt like the breath had been punched from her lungs. She was unable even to scream as the figures stepped forward into the light. The man was tall and skinny with a razor-sharp moustache, smooth black hair, and dark eyes that seemed to glitter. The woman beside him was slender and wore her black hair in a sleek bob.

"So," said the man in a deep, clipped voice. "We have found you at last."

The woman nodded. "Now we can do what we came here to do."

Together, they started down the stairs. . . .

Chapter Twenty-nine

J ess looked back down at Skribble and the book on her lap—and found that both had gone. She gasped, turned to Michael . . . in time to find him slipping the book inside his robe. In a daze she realized he must have snatched it the second he saw the genies.

Now the man and the woman had reached the bottom of the stairs.

"Stay away from us," said Milly, her voice wavering. "Or I'll scream, and my dad and mum will come and get you and—"

"No one will hear your screams, child," said the woman, her voice as cold and jagged as icicles. "We have drawn a veil of silence around your parents' room. They will hear nothing beyond it."

Michael grabbed Milly's hand and squeezed it tightly. "What do you want?"

The woman narrowed her eyes. "You have in your possession things that do not belong here."

"No, we don't," protested Michael.

"*You lie!*" boomed the man, his eyes burning. "I am Sabik, and my companion is Vega. We have journeyed from the Genie Realm. We have traced the magical emanations of the handbook—it is useless to lie to us about what you have and do not have."

If Sabik had a fiery temper, the woman, Vega, was more like frost. "We want the book back now," she said coldly. "We know you have it. Return it to us."

A strangled squeak of alarm came from the direction of Michael's robe. He hastily coughed.

"NOW!" Sabik thundered.

Jess found the courage to speak. "No!"

"You dare defy us?" Vega exclaimed.

"We can do magic, too," said Milly fiercely. "We've been *training*."

"Fools," snapped Sabik. "Meddle no more with the great mysteries. It is not for human infants to train as genies!" He held out his hand. "Surrender the book and your lamp at once!"

"And make no attempt to deceive us," Vega warned. "We will detect the magic around the lamp. We will know if you have been inside it."

Jess was about to retort that the lamp wasn't even down here in the den, when Jason stood up, his legs trembling.

"All right," he said. "If you want the lamp, you can have it."

"No—" Michael began.

Then he saw that Jason had picked up the duck flashlight!

Jason slowly crossed the den to give it to the genie couple.

Sabik sneered. "What monstrosity is this?"

"It's . . . it's a modern lamp," stammered Jason, his palms sweating. Vega swept it from his hand.

A frown crossed her beautiful face as she studied the flashlight. "The child speaks the truth, Sabik. Primitive magic surrounds this lamp. I can tell a trainee has been inside it."

"He abuses our craft." Sabik frowned. "I must cleanse this lamp from within." He spoke strange-sounding words and a haze of yellow light engulfed him. Then he shrank and spiraled into the flashlight.

A moment later a deep cry of anger echoed around the room and blue sparks erupted from the plastic duck.

Vega dropped the flashlight and backed away. "What trickery is this?" she exclaimed in alarm.

Michael saw their chance. "Everyone up the stairs!" he yelled. "NOW!"

Milly grabbed Jason by the hand and fled up the stairs

with him. Michael and Jess made to follow as Sabik suddenly burst back into being at the bottom of the staircase.

But he was stuck—hunched over and helpless, just as Jason had been! Vega crouched to help her companion.

Jess jumped over them both. "Come on!" Clutching the book tightly beneath his robe, Michael did the same.

"Stop the humans, Vega!" Sabik shouted.

Vega pointed to the top of the stairs. The door swung shut.

But Michael and Jess had already thrown themselves through it, just in time.

"Where's the real lamp?" Michael gasped.

"Beside my bed!" Jess was already sprinting for the stairs in the hall.

As they took them three at a time, they could hear Milly and Jason trying to open the door to their parents' bedroom.

"It's stuck!" Jason cried. "Locked or something."

"Wake up!" Milly shouted. "We're all in danger!"

"They can't hear you," Michael yelled. "Veil of silence, remember?"

Jason nodded. "I know. I just thought . . ." He shrugged, close to tears. "I don't know what I thought!"

Michael's voice softened. "Hey," he said. "That trick

with the duck flashlight, that was brilliant, Jase. That was inspired!"

Milly nodded. "I can't believe Sabik went inside it."

"I wasn't expecting him to," Jason admitted. "I just thought he might believe that was the real lamp and leave us alone."

"*I've* got the real one," Jess cried, bursting from her bedroom.

"And I've still got the book," said Michael. He pulled it out as he ran along the landing to join her, the others close behind. "Skribble? You okay?"

The bookworm stuck out his trembling head. "We must flee! That trick won't delay them for long!"

They heard an ominous thump from downstairs as the door to the den was thrown open. "You will never escape!" Sabik was roaring. "Now that we have finally traced the book, we can follow it anywhere—however fast you flee."

Jason looked dismayed. "Vega must have unstuck him."

"And now they're in the hall," Milly realized. "And we're trapped up here!"

"No, we're not," said Jess. "We just need to use some magic ourselves! Jason, quick—get in the lamp!"

Jason nodded. "Genie me!"

He swooshed away into the cold brass spout. Jess rubbed the lamp and he emerged a moment later in a puff of green smoke and full genie gear, his turban spotlessly white, his slippers extra curly, and his moustache neatly groomed. "What is your wish?" he boomed.

Jess lifted her chin. "I wish that you, me, Milly, and Michael could *fly away* through the window to the middle of Moreham Wood!"

"As you say!" Jason grinned and clapped his hands grandly. The glass vanished from the windowpanes. And the next moment, all four of them started rising slowly into the air!

"I don't believe it!" breathed Michael.

Milly squealed. "We're flying!"

Jess felt a moment's panic as she found herself moving with the others toward the window. But then suddenly she was soaring through the sky in her satin pajamas, clutching the lamp tightly. Her fear faded away as she gave herself up to the incredible feeling. She was weightless, blown like a feather through the chilly morning, looking down at the garden far below and the pointed tops of the conifer trees. Magic had never seemed more special or intense.

Then, all too soon, Jess found herself slowly dropping down into the heart of Moreham Wood. Her bare feet hit the cold, muddy ground and she almost slipped over.

She felt heavy and clumsy, holding the lamp so tightly her fingertips had turned white.

"That was amazing," said Milly, landing neatly on a pile of leaves in her furry rabbit slippers.

Jason nodded. "Let's do it again!"

"Wish us farther away, Jess," Michael urged her, shivering in the thin daylight. "This is too close to the house. They'll find us again."

Jess nodded and opened her mouth—but no sound came out. She gasped and wheezed, but couldn't form a single word.

"Jess?" said Jason, concerned. "What's up?"

Skribble pushed his way out of the split in the book's cover, butting Michael in the ribs with his head. "Sabik and Vega must know that she made the wish," he cried. "They have taken her voice so she can wish no more."

Milly rushed to Jess and hugged her. "Oh, no! Poor Jess!"

"And Jason can't be freed unless Jess says so," Michael realized. "We're helpless again!"

Jess shook her head, gave Milly the lamp, then dug her finger into the muddy ground and started to write: G . . . E . . . N . . . I . . . E . . .

"She's writing down the release words!" Milly realized.

Jason looked at Skribble. "Will that work?"

"It had better," said Michael.

Jason shot back up the spout of the lamp and waited.

Jess concentrated hard. As she scrawled in the mud, she wished as hard as she could that Jason would burst back out of the lamp in his blue pajamas, normal again. . . .

"B . . . E . . . F . . ." Michael was reading each letter aloud. "R . . . E . . . E!"

Even as he spoke the last letter, Jason was blown back out of the spout and went staggering into a tree.

"Jess, you did it!" Milly cried, embracing her again, and Jason grinned gratefully.

"Nonverbal lamp control," said Skribble approvingly. "A clear sign of natural magical ability."

Michael looked around. A noise had started up in the distance. It sounded like someone crashing through the woods. "They know we're in here," he said grimly. "Jess, get in the lamp."

She frowned at him, pointing to her mouth. He pointed back at the ground. With a sigh, Jess bent back over and used her muddy finger to daub, *GENIE ME!*

With a soundless gasp of surprise she was tugged feet-first into the spout of the lamp. Milly rubbed it and Jess came back out again in a shower of silver glitter. She was wearing her cutoff top, tiara, gold sandals—and a big black puffer jacket. Michael looked surprised. "It's cold!" she mouthed at him.

"I wish Jess had her voice back!" said Milly.

Jess clicked her fingers—and gasped out loud. "Thank goodness for that!"

Michael shushed her furiously; the crashing sounds were getting closer. "Okay, Milly, wish us away somewhere."

"Shall we go flying again?" Milly asked.

"They'll spot us in the air," said Jason worriedly. "Although, I guess if they've got magic vision, they can spot us wandering around anywhere."

"Maybe not *anywhere*," Milly replied with a crafty smile. "I wish we were all tiny and hiding in an underground tunnel beneath the woods!"

"As you command," said Jess, wriggling her fingers.

Michael felt a weird, spinning sensation, and his stomach lurched like he was caught in an invisible lift, moving from the top floor to the basement at incredible speed. In a sprinkling of silver stardust, everything went dark, and he and the others found themselves all bunched up together. There was a thick, cold, earthy smell in the air, and it was pitch-black. Michael clutched the book close to him. He tried to stand up straight but banged his head on the muddy roof.

"Oh, lovely," Michael complained. His voice sounded loud and strangely deadened by the thick walls of earth. "How tall are we?"

"I was aiming for the size of a pencil," said Jess. "But it's too dark to really tell."

"I wish there was some light in here!" Milly said.

With a clap of magic hands, Jess conjured a small light-bulb. It stuck out of the mud roof and gave off a strong, steady light.

"I went for a sixty-watt bulb," Jess explained. "Is that okay, or would you prefer a hundred-watt one?"

"All right, Miss Show-off!" Michael complained.

"Milly," said Jason, "can't you wish that they won't ever be able to find us?"

"That would never work," said Skribble. "We would need to know the full extent of those two genies' abilities to be able to limit their powers."

"And I can't see them telling us even if we *were* dumb enough to ask," said Michael. "But we're not giving up. We're *not*. We've come so far. It's not fair that we can't finish the genie training!"

"You heard what Skribble said—and Sabik," said Jess quietly. "We were never meant to start it. And when you look at some of the things that have gone wrong . . ."

"But we can't just hand over the lamp, the book, and

Skribble," Milly protested.

Skribble nodded vigorously. "Quite so, Milly!"

"Hang on, Jess," said Michael. "Maybe some things went wrong, but we've managed to put a lot of things right, too. Maybe we can use some of the stuff we've learned." He pointed to Jason. "I mean, that stuff with the flashlight—you gave the genies what they wanted back in the den, but you twisted it so things went wrong for them—just like you did with Foxtrot. And, Jess, you've always been good at illusions. You were the best at making food, and look at the way you gave yourself that coat just now. . . ."

Jess frowned. "So?"

Michael picked up two clods of soil. "Could you transform these into an identical lamp and a handbook to go with it?"

"Decoys!" said Jason excitedly. "To fool the genies."

Michael beamed. "Exactly!"

"Make another book first," Skribble said hastily. "It is I that they truly seek. They must have been hunting me for centuries. . . ." His voice rose in a wail. "And now they will imprison me forever!"

"We won't let that happen," declared Milly.

Jess bit her lip. "Show me the book."

Michael passed it to her. "Don't just look at it, Jess. *Feel* it. Think of the way it tingles and shakes . . . the way it smells so old . . . you have to get this right."

Jess closed her eyes and, running her fingers over the book, remembered the way she had felt when she'd first touched it. Its image seemed to shine in her mind.

Milly passed the lamp to Jason and took one of the clods of earth. "I wish we had an exact copy of *The Genie Handbook*," she whispered.

"As you wish!" Jess boomed, sending showers of soil from the roof. When she opened her eyes, she saw Milly gazing down in delight at an identical copy of the book in her hand.

"That's amazing, Jess," she said, opening it up. "The paper looks just right, and the ink, too! Even the cracks in the leather . . ."

Jess gave a relieved smile and passed the real handbook back to Michael.

"Hey," marveled Milly, "this fake even shakes like the real thing."

"It's not the book that's shaking," said Michael as vibrations shuddered through the ground. "It's the whole tunnel!"

The lightbulb began to flicker, and more soil loosened

from the low ceiling.

"Something is approaching," hissed Skribble, ducking hastily back down inside the real book.

Jason gulped. "The genies must have found us again!"

The children huddled together as a huge, grotesque shadow appeared at the far end of the tunnel.

Chapter Thirty

"It's a monster!" yelled Milly.

"No." Michael was staring down the tunnel in amazement. "It's . . . it's a *mole*. Look, it's a giant mole!"

Jason shook his head. "It's a normal-size mole. We're tiny down here, remember?"

Huge pink nose twitching, dark matted fur glinting in the flickering light, the gigantic mole filled the tunnel as it made its way blindly toward them.

Michael frowned. "What a weird thing to attack us with!"

"It's *not* actually attacking," Jess observed. "Maybe it's just an ordinary mole passing through."

"It can still squash us flat, though," cried Jason. "Come on, Milly—*wish*!"

Milly was seized by sudden inspiration. "I wish my rabbit slippers were real, normal-size rabbits!"

"As you command!" Jess hollered.

Milly squealed as two rabbits shot up from the ground

and filled the tunnel completely. They faced the mole, sniffing it as it approached, blocking its way. The mole sniffed them back with a wet snuffling sound.

Michael raised an eyebrow. "Clash of the titans," he said dryly.

"Maybe the genies wanted the mole to herd us back down the tunnel," Jason reasoned. "Maybe they've set a trap there!"

"I wish one of the rabbits would burrow its way back up to the surface," said Milly breathlessly. Jess snapped her fingers, and in a flash of light the rabbit duly obeyed, kicking up a huge amount of earth in its wake. The whole tunnel seemed ready to come crashing down on top of them before the giant bunny disappeared from view.

"What did you do that for, Mil?" said Michael angrily, brushing huge crumbs of earth from the real book.

Milly smiled slyly. "Because now, Sabik and Vega will think we've followed the rabbit out through that tunnel into the woods and go looking there—when *really* I'm going to wish us somewhere else!"

"Okay, that *is* pretty clever," Michael conceded.

"Michael, why don't you be genie?" said Jess. "You took us to London that time and you got us back again in a tin can. I think you're best at going long distances." She scooted back into the lamp.

"Genie be free," said Milly, and Jess was catapulted back into the tunnel—without her coat and barefoot again. The remaining mega-bunny jumped in surprise, startling the mole, who scurried away from them back down the tunnel.

Michael gave Jess the real book and said, "Genie me!"

Jason quickly rubbed the side of the lamp. A moment later, Michael reappeared in his traditional cloud of smoke, wearing his huge beard and black ninja-style outfit.

"Ah, that's better," he said, looking at his feet. "Fur-lined slippers."

Jess nudged Jason. "Get on with it!"

"I wish we were . . ." Jason shrugged. "I wish we were all back to our normal size on a desert island in the South Pacific!"

"Gotcha," said Michael.

There was a red flash of light, and then the world plunged into dizzying darkness. Jason kept tight hold of the lamp as he felt himself tumbling over and over and over. . . .

But then suddenly his bare feet were half-buried in warm sand. Blazing sunshine prickled his skin. Opening his eyes, he found himself on a spotless stretch of white beach. A clear, deep blue sea lapped at the shore.

"Michael, you did it!" he exclaimed.

"Pretty cool, huh?" said Michael, grinning. "It's one of the Cook Islands, I think. We did them in geography. Some bloke lived alone here for ten years."

Jess pointed grimly across the water. "I think our stay is going to be a bit shorter."

Two specks had appeared on the horizon and were getting steadily closer.

"Oh, no," breathed Jason, a familiar fear building inside him.

Sabik and Vega were gliding across the ocean toward them, as if standing on invisible surfboards.

"They've found us already!" said Milly despairingly. "I *didn't* put them off our trail after all!"

"Of course you didn't!" called Skribble from inside the book. "Every time magic is performed in this world, it leaves a mark, a trace, a trail. That is how this evil genie pair tracked the book down in the first place—with every step of training that you have passed, the magic trails it leaves have grown stronger. Now they shine out like bright beacons for Sabik and Vega to follow."

Jess watched as the genies drew nearer. "But if they can follow our trail of magic," she cried, "we'll *never* be able to escape them!"

Michael had an idea. "What if we left lots of trails—*false* trails? Then they wouldn't know which way to go."

"Quick!" Milly urged them. The two genies were so close now that she could see their eyes glinting in the sunlight.

Jason nodded excitedly. "I wish that when we next use magic to travel, we leave a million magical paths leading in all directions to Mars and back!"

"Excellent wish!" thundered Michael.

Jess stuffed the real *Genie Handbook* up her pajama top, grabbed the decoy she had made for Milly, and hurled it with all her strength into the sea. "Fetch!" she yelled, and was gladdened to see Sabik and Vega veer off in hot pursuit of the book—buying Jason time.

"I wish we were in Mum and Mark's bookshop," he whispered.

"Here we go!" Michael shouted. His beard glowed electric blue, and suddenly bright sparks of light seemed to shoot out of him, whip-cracking across the clear sky for miles in all directions.

Jason grabbed hold of Milly for support as Michael's genie magic sent the world tumbling again, like they were all caught inside a whirlpool. Jason felt himself falling through space, sucked down into nothingness. . . .

Then, with a sickening jerk, he found himself stumbling into a bookcase and collapsing amid a hail of paperbacks.

"We made it," Jess groaned, flat on her back in the

romantic fiction aisle. Milly sat beside her, clutching her head. Jess pulled the handbook from beneath her top and laid it carefully on Milly's lap.

Michael turned sharply to Jason. "What made you bring us here?"

"There's a saying," said Jason, getting cautiously to his feet. "Where better to hide a tree than in a forest?"

Milly looked alarmed. "You're not going to wish we were all trees, are you?"

"No. But look around," said Jason. "What do you see?"

"Tons of old books," said Jess. Then she smiled. "Of course! Who would notice one more old book among this lot!"

"I thought we could hide the real handbook here, then wish ourselves somewhere else," Jason explained, looking around the shelves for a likely slot. "By the time those genies realize the book in the sea isn't the *real* book, untangle all the magical trails we left behind, and work out where we've gone, Skribble might just have had time to think of a way to get us all out of this."

"I *have* been thinking," came Skribble's muffled tones. Milly opened the book and out he popped, looking very sorry for himself. "Your plan is good . . . but doomed to failure."

Michael threw his beard over his shoulder impatiently. "What're you on about, Worm?"

"I mean that whatever we do, we cannot hide forever," said Skribble. "You have bought us all valuable time . . . but Sabik and Vega will track us down. It is inevitable."

Jess felt suddenly weary as she noticed the clock on the wall. "Look at the time. Six forty in the morning. All that effort, and we've only been on the run for about fifteen minutes!"

Jason's face paled. "Fifteen minutes? It feels more like fifteen days!"

"Look on the bright side," said Michael moodily. "If we *are* zapped into magic dust, we won't be able to come to Dad and Ann's boring opening party!"

"That's not funny," Jess snapped.

"Well," said Milly firmly. "If we can't get away from Sabik and Vega . . . we'll have to get Sabik and Vega away from *us*. If only we could put them back in their lamps— they'd have to stay in there then, until someone summoned them!"

For a few moments, no one spoke as her words sank in.

Jason smiled at her. "Milly . . . that's brilliant!"

Skribble looked up from the book, frowning. "You know, even as you spoke, Milly, I had hit upon that very same plan—to send them back to their lamps by using your human-genie magic!"

"The worm's nicking your idea, Mil," said Michael, giving her a thumbs-up. "Must be a winner."

"But hang on, our magic only lasts until sunset," Jason said. "Then they'll be free again!"

"No!" said Jess. "Remember when Michael was stuck inside the lamp in Ollie's room? Skribble said he might be stuck there forever!"

Skribble nodded excitedly. "No genie, whether trainee or master, can emerge from his lamp until the spell of release is said or the vessel is rubbed. If you can get the genies into their lamps, then it doesn't matter that your magic will wear off at sunset—they will be held there by the ancient laws of geniedom!"

"Get wishing then, Jase," said Michael, "and I'll get stuffing those genies back in their lamps!"

"The task is beyond you, my boy," Skribble told him. "It is beyond any single one of you to perform. These genies are extremely powerful."

"They've been pretty soft on us so far," Michael argued. "They haven't killed us or anything."

"They're toying with us," said Jason darkly. "I bet they just want to get Skribble and the book back safely—then they're *really* going to punish us."

Milly sat down heavily beside a case of secondhand

crime novels. "But what are we going to do? If one of us can't do it—"

"—maybe all *four* of us can." Jess looked around at Michael, Milly, and Jason. "I mean, right from the start, we know the book's been judging us all together."

"A sort of group-genie," Jason agreed.

Michael clicked his fingers. "Maybe, somehow, if we could all get into the lamp together . . ."

"Then Skribble could rub the lamp and bring us *all* out as genies!" Milly cried.

"Four times the power!" said Jess.

Jason turned to Skribble. "Would that work? Do you think we could do it?"

The book had already started to tremble, and Milly quickly set it down on the floor. "My tail's tingling!" gasped Skribble. "Yes, I . . . I think the book agrees! You, Michael—revert to your usual dreary appearance at once. Everyone must start the spell in the same state."

Michael spiraled off back inside the lamp. "Genie be free," commanded Jason.

In the blink of an eye, Michael was back. "Come on, then!"

Skribble looked at them. "You all know what to do?"

"Yes," said Jess, and the others nodded. Jason set the lamp down on the floor beside Skribble. Then he joined

Michael, Jess, and Milly, standing a small distance away, facing the lamp.

Each of them took a deep, deep breath.

"Genie us!" they shouted.

Michael caught a crazy corkscrew glimpse of the others whizzing through the air, shrinking in size just as he was, as the lamp's spout loomed up like the mouth of a bright brass dragon. They circled down inside its musty, metallic belly until at last they lay still, panting on the hard floor.

"Okay," said Michael, picking himself up. He held out both hands. "Are we gonna do this?"

Without hesitation, Jess reached out and took his hand. Michael took Milly's, and she and Jess took Jason's.

"We're up for the challenge," Jason said, no waver in his voice.

"We can do it," Milly declared. "I know we can."

Then, before anyone could say another word, they felt a warm, swirling sensation and were sucked back up into the air and spat out through the spout, still holding hands. They made a perfect landing beside the cash register in a swirl of magnificent pinky-gray smoke and a slew of silver sparks.

Skribble was watching from beside the lamp. It might have been Milly's imagination, but she thought she saw a glimmer of pride in his beady eyes.

"What is your wish?" Milly asked the bookworm, in perfect time with Michael, Jason, and Jess.

"I wish that you would cast Sabik and Vega back into their lamps," Skribble cried, "wherever they may be!"

"Your wish is our command," boomed the four genies-in-training.

Milly closed her eyes and pictured Sabik and Vega. She felt power flowing into her fingertips from Michael and Jason, and sent energy of her own back to them and to Jess. It was a wonderful, intoxicating feeling. *We can do anything,* she thought. *Together, we really can!*

In her mind, she pictured the two dark-eyed genies. Then she placed two lamps beside them, blurry at first but hardening into focus. She heard Michael, Jess, and Jason speaking in her head, and added her own voice to the chant. "Go back . . . go back. . . . Back to your lamp you must go. . . . *Back to your lamp you must go!*"

"It's working!" Skribble said in delight. "Yes, it's working."

I know it's working, thought Milly dreamily. *I can feel it working.*

"Good children! Fine, upstanding, *out*standing children!" Skribble kept babbling on and on. "Of course, you are highly fortunate to have had as fine a teacher as me, someone who saw your potential and . . ." Abruptly, his voice dropped to a shocked whisper. "Oh, no . . . *no* . . . !"

"What's wrong?" Milly asked, opening her eyes.

"Stop, children!" squawked Skribble, staring at them in alarm. "You must stop!"

"Stop?" Michael shook his head. "Too late. We've already done it!"

"But *what* have we done?" breathed Jess.

Suddenly, Milly realized that Skribble was looking *past* them, and that Jess was staring in the same direction. She swung around.

And saw a small, brass vase rocking slowly to and fro. No, not a vase, she realized. A *lamp*. A lamp that was being *used* as a vase. She stared in horror as it started to rock faster and faster.

As if there was something trapped inside.

Something angry.

The two orange flowers stuffed in the spout of the lamp withered and crumbled to dust. The dust spiraled in the air and started to thicken into smoke.

"We sent the evil genies back to their lamps, all right," whispered Jason, transfixed. "We just never imagined one of their lamps was *here in the shop with us all the time.*"

"So what? They can't get out if we don't rub the

lamp," said Milly. "Can they?"

"It looks like no one's told *them* that!" Michael's voice rose with panic as the smoke began to take the shape of a tall, thin woman.

The children backed away as Vega shimmered into view, her eyes dark and glittering in her beautiful face.

"Give up this contest," she warned them. "You can never escape from us. Never!"

As the children stared, horrified, Vega turned and softly caressed the brass lamp on the shelf beside her. "Come forth, Sabik!"

In a flash of red light, Sabik burst from inside it. He seemed bigger and broader than before, his moustache thicker and greased into curls at each end. He was holding another, smaller lamp—bright gold and studded with colorful jewels, which he passed to Vega. She took it and stroked it tenderly.

"That must be *her* lamp," Michael realized, turning to Sabik. "You were carrying it around with you all the time—so when we sent you into your own lamps, all you had to do was rub hers to set her free."

"Naturally." Sabik smiled coldly. "Since I was separated from my own lamp, carrying Vega's was a sensible precaution. Would you not agree?"

"I don't agree with anything!" shouted Milly, too

terrified even to cry. "I don't get it! How come your lamp was here in the shop?"

"It was Mum!" Jess said in a breathless whisper. "Remember she said she'd bought something in Junk and Disorderly that same day we did? *That's* what she must have bought—Sabik's lamp!" She remembered the parcel Vega had been carrying in the junk shop. "That day we first saw you—you sold Sabik's lamp to Barry, the owner, didn't you? But why?"

"It was a trap," Vega said simply. "We had been waiting for so many centuries in the Genie Realm, for the handbook's magic to be awoken. When at last it was, we followed the faint glimmer of its magic to your settlement here. The magic was too weak for us to track the book precisely. However, we knew that the first thing the book instructs its students to attain is . . ."

"A worthy vessel," breathed Milly. "A lamp!"

Jess nodded. "So you left Sabik's lamp in the junk shop because you knew it was just the sort of place a trainee human genie would search for one."

Jason looked at Jess. "If we'd bought it and tried to get inside, Sabik would have known straightaway!"

"Yes," Sabik agreed. "You would have been caught as surely as a fly in amber. And with a single wish from Vega we would have come to you and taken our prize . . .

282

that for which we have spent nearly two thousand years searching. . . ."

Hidden behind the lamp, Skribble gave a low moan of fear. Then he dived into the book and back out of sight.

"But your plan didn't work, did it?" Jess said, looking at the genies. "We got to the shop before you."

"And, unlucky for you, there was already a lamp there," Michael chipped in.

Jess nodded. "We bought it and left just as you arrived, so you had to start looking for us the hard way."

"That is so," Sabik boomed. "We watched and waited for the magic to guide us. The trails grew stronger. We followed them. Three times, we saw you at places where magic had been cast—but never once with a lamp. And so we bided our time, waiting to be sure we had the right people. . . ."

"Time has little meaning for us," said Vega. "But the same cannot be said for you, little humans. Your lives are over so quickly. . . ."

The genies walked slowly toward them. . . .

Chapter Thirty-one

"Stay away from us," Jess warned them in a shaky voice.

"Yeah, leave us alone!" Michael snatched up the book and hugged it to his chest. "Just 'cause Skribble is good and you're evil!"

"Skribble?" Vega frowned, halted her advance.

"We know you're evil!" said Milly. "We know you want to punish us for doing magic."

"Silly child, we have no real quarrel with you," said Sabik. "Why do you suppose we sent a harmless burrowing creature to pursue you below the ground?"

"The mole," Michael realized.

"You used the power of the book but you did so innocently," said Vega. "You are but an irritation to be swept aside. We desire only to take back that which is ours."

"I don't care!" Milly said. "Skribble isn't yours, and you can't have him!"

Jason nodded. "You can take our lamp, but you can't

have the book *or* Skribble."

"Not unless you're prepared to come through all of us first," agreed Michael grimly.

"Skribble? Who is this Skribble?" Suddenly Sabik began to smile. "Surely, you cannot mean . . ."

Vega looked at him and smiled too. "Skribbaleum? Skribbaleum El Lazeez Ekir—after all this time?"

Sabik boomed with laughter. "Well, well! So *this* is where he ended up."

"What are you talking about?" said Michael nervously.

"You infants really think we have been after . . . *him*?" Vega shook her head, her gaze lingering on the book in Michael's arms. "That is the only prize we seek. A humble book for genie children . . . but the final volume needed to complete the rebuilding of the Great Genie Library of Magical Muses."

Skribble popped up through a hole in the cover. "What are you talking about?" His specklike eyes were as wide as they would go. "Don't be ridiculous! You are looking for *me*; of course you are!"

Sabik laughed louder than ever. "You were ever a miserable worm in spirit—now you are one in body, too! How could *you* possibly interest us, Skribbaleum El Lazeez Ekir?" His eyes glittered contemptuously. "As a genie you

285

were incompetent, lazy, and shirked your duties."

Skribble gasped. "No—"

"It is true, and you know it," Vega snapped. "You are nothing!"

In front of everyone's eyes, Skribble's body seemed to deflate as if he was a balloon stuck with a pin.

"Don't be so mean!" Milly shouted at the genies. "Leave him alone!"

"Yeah, Skribble was a *great* genie," Jason said loyally. "He told us he was!"

The genie couple both looked at Skribble.

A piteous moan broke from the little bookworm's mouth.

"Skribble?" Jess said uncertainly.

Milly crouched down. "What are they talking about? Please tell us. I know you weren't completely honest about wanting us to help you, but—"

"You *were* a great genie . . ." said Jason, "weren't you?"

Skribble whimpered.

Michael and Jess exchanged looks over Milly's and Jason's heads. Jess hesitated and then knelt by Milly. "Skribble, it doesn't matter if you've been lying," she said, glancing back at Michael, who gave a brief nod. "Just tell us the truth now. We need to know. What's going on?"

There was silence.

"Well, Skribbaleum?" Vega said. "Do you not think these children who champion you have a right to know?"

Skribble lifted his head. "Perhaps . . . I didn't tell you . . . the whole truth. I *could* have been a great genie." He glanced warily at the couple, as if waiting for them to contradict him, but Vega nodded slightly. "I had more natural magical ability than any of the other genies, but I . . . I squandered that gift." The worm took a deep breath. "Remember I told you that I had done nothing to deserve being locked up?"

They nodded.

"Well, I suppose I *really* meant that I deserved being locked up because I had done nothing. Nothing at all!" He cringed with shame. "I was lazy. I took shortcuts. I granted shoddy wishes."

Michael couldn't believe it. "All the stuff you've been moaning at us for!"

"I was warned. Time and again I was warned," Skribble went on. "But I did not heed those warnings. And then, at the mighty Sultan Alishka's seventieth birthday party . . ." The little worm shuddered at the memory. "The great sultan was granted a wish from every genie in the Realm. Of myself, he wished that he could seat himself upon solid gold, wherever and whenever he went."

"Sort of like a portable throne?" Michael considered. "Sounds like that wish would've taken some planning."

"Indeed, it would have," Sabik boomed. "But you had no interest in planning, did you, Skribbaleum? So you simply turned the sultan's own *bottom* into gold!"

"Oh, Skribble," Jess said.

"It was what he wished for!" Skribble argued. "Wherever he sat, he sat on gold!"

Vega nodded. "But soon he sat upon a judge's throne, did he not?"

"Yes. I was found guilty of laziness and irresponsibility," said Skribble, so quietly the children had to strain to hear. "The Genie High Council stripped me of my magic powers and compelled me to spend one hundred years locked in the great genie library, rereading, relearning, and inwardly digesting the wisdom from the books there. They decreed that after this time, I would regain some of my powers— but my full magic would not return until I helped someone achieve his heart's desire."

"You *said* you were locked away!" Jason remembered. "But we thought you meant by evil genies."

Skribble looked ashamed as he nodded. "I let you believe that."

"But why?" Milly whispered. "Why didn't you tell us the truth?"

"I . . ." Skribble hesitated and then looked up at her. "I had come to . . . to *like* you." He started weeping softly. "I did not want you to think badly of me."

"Oh, Skribble." Milly gently wiped away the tears with her little finger. "You should have just told us."

Jess nodded. "We'd have understood."

"*I* wouldn't have," Michael grunted.

"Ignore him," said Milly. "You wouldn't believe how many teachers have wanted to lock *him* up."

"So, what happened?" Jason asked Skribble. "How did you come to be in the book? Did you really magic yourself inside it?"

Skribble nodded. "But not for the reason I told you. I was furious with the High Council for believing they could punish me. *Me!*" For a moment a familiar look of pride flashed across his face. "I decided that since they had told me to digest the books, I would do *exactly* that—and so I used the last of my magic to transform myself into a bookworm."

Jason grinned. "So you could eat the books and *really* digest them!"

An impressed smile flickered across Michael's face, too. "Okay, that's actually quite smart, Worm."

Skribble nodded, almost smugly. "As the decades went by I fulfilled the terms of my punishment, eating my way through book after book. . . ."

"It took centuries to repair the damage you caused," rumbled Sabik.

Skribble gave him a defiant look. "I was chomping quite happily through *The Genie Handbook* when the library was ransacked and I was taken far away!"

"Hundreds of books were stolen that day," said Sabik, his eyes clouding at the memory. "Many of them so magical they could alter the very fabric of human reality."

Vega nodded. "Recovering those volumes took priority over a simple beginner's guide to geniedom."

Skribble looked at her. "And as the centuries passed and I slept, you genies, you . . ." A fat tear squeezed out of his left eye. "You all *forgot* me."

Sabik nodded, his face impassive as ever. "People live on in the memory through their achievements, Skribbaleum. In your life as a genie, you achieved nothing worth remembering."

"But when the handbook was stolen, why didn't you change back to your true self?" Jason asked. "Why did you stay as a bookworm?"

Skribble sighed. "I have already told you, boy, I used the last of my magic to assume this shape! I will not be able to transform myself back until all my powers return, and that will only happen when—"

"You grant someone his heart's desire," Milly realized.

"So that was your plan!" It all suddenly made sense to Jason. "That's why you made us vow that our heart's desire was to be genies, before we started our training."

Michael nodded. "You thought if we got through the training and *became* genies, you'd get back your magic and your freedom!"

Vega looked around at the children. "I am forced to admit the four of you have shown great aptitude for a magical existence in your attempts to evade us."

"You showed courage and spirit when you ignored the book's final instruction that it was safer to do nothing," said Sabik. "By choosing to stand against us, you made the decision to fashion your own fates, just as you did when first you gave the book that memorable command—'Genie us.'" He smiled. "This pleases us."

Jess blinked. "It does?"

"Wait a sec, how do you know about us saying, 'Genie us'?" Michael demanded.

Vega smiled at him, and the glitter in her eyes seemed suddenly more like the twinkling of the stars at night than the glint of ice. "Magic," she said softly.

And as she spoke, the handbook shook and fell open in Michael's hands. He gasped and held it out as the pages flicked over. They stopped.

"Your labors are complete," murmured Vega. "Behold, the judgment of the book."

Michael stared down at the yellowed pages. For a few seconds, he held himself completely rigid. Then he held it out to Jess, Jason, and Milly for them all to see.

The Genie Handbook

Verdict:

You have passed.

Chapter Thirty-two

The words stood out boldly on the page, in ink as black as the depths of space.

"We've passed?" Jess breathed. "But . . . but that means we're . . ."

"Genies!" Michael whispered.

The four of them looked at each other in shock.

"Really?" said Milly, her hands flying to her mouth. "We're really proper genies?"

Vega shook her head. "Not quite."

"What do you mean?" asked Jason.

"The book says that you have passed," said Sabik. "Which means that you can *become* genies, should you wish it."

"Well, of course we do!" Michael said impatiently.

"Yeah," said Milly, "we want to be able to do proper magic."

"Magic that doesn't fade at sunset," Jess added.

"You may do all that in time." Sabik smiled, his dark

eyes glittering. "But first you must leave the human world behind."

His words were like a cold wind gusting into the shop.

Jess's skin prickled with goose bumps. "What . . . what do you mean?"

"Before you can become full genies, we must know if humans make worthy vessels for such knowledge," Vega explained. "And so we must take you from this world to the Genie Realm."

"Well . . . how long would we be away for?" Jess asked.

"Not long," Sabik told her. "You all show great promise. Perhaps . . . two or three hundred years?"

There was a long silence.

"But humans don't even live that long!" Jason protested.

"*You* would," said Vega.

Michael glowered at Sabik and Vega. "You genies really have a laugh, don't you? With all your loopholes and your tricks . . . What it boils down to is that after all we've been through, after all the effort we've put into passing all the different steps, unless we go off and live in Genie Land with you we get *nothing*!"

"I didn't know this, children, I promise," Skribble murmured. "I am so sorry."

"You baffle me, infants," said Vega. "Did you not tell the book that your heart's desire was to become genies?"

"Skribble made us say that," Jess said. "But our hearts' desire was really to get back to London."

Sabik looked at her shrewdly. "Was it indeed?"

"I see." Vega's eyes glinted. "Are we to understand that you are rejecting our invitation to travel to the Genie Realm?"

Michael nodded. "We can't go."

"We don't want to," said Milly more firmly.

"I couldn't leave Mum and Mark," said Jason. "I just couldn't."

"None of us could," Jess affirmed.

Sabik's face darkened. "You deny yourselves the glory we could give you?"

"Please don't be angry with them," Skribble begged the genies. "These children are only human. They have small minds, but such big hearts. . . . Let them be, great Sabik. Please, merciful Vega, let them be!" The words spilled out of him. "It is I who have led the children astray. It was my folly—if anyone must be punished, let it be me, not them!"

"So . . ." Sabik surveyed the bookworm coldly. "Humility and compassion at last, Skribbaleum?"

Skribble hung his head miserably.

"Very well, so be it." Sabik brushed his hands briskly together. "If the human infants choose to reject the chance we are offering them, then we accept it." He turned back to the children. "You have found *The Genie Handbook* and brought our search to an end. According to custom, you must be given something in exchange. If you will not accept a privileged place in the Genie Realm, then we shall grant you one wish."

"One each?" Michael asked hopefully.

"One to share," said Vega. "Use it wisely."

"Then . . . we could do it," Jess realized, looking at Michael, Milly, and Jason. "Put things back. Go to London, have our old lives again. We could make the wish and have what we've always wanted."

For a long moment they all just looked at each other.

"Oh, Jess . . ." cried Milly, breaking the silence first. "I'm sorry, but I don't think I *do* want it anymore! I don't care if we can't do magic; I don't care if I don't get any more wishes. I'll try to be neater and not mess up our room, and not to annoy you so much, but I . . ." She shrugged. "I like it here in Moreways Meet. I want to go riding with Emily and to drama club and . . . and I want us all to live together like we do now."

"Know what?" Michael suddenly crossed to his sister and put his arm around her. "I don't want to go either."

Jess and Jason looked at him in astonishment.

Michael shrugged. "This place has grown on me, okay? So my mobile might not have a signal here, but I can always ask for a different phone for my birthday. Karate was cool last night. School's not bad and . . ." He looked away, his cheeks flushing slightly. "Well, I guess I'm with Mil. It's good, us all living in one place."

"Yeah," said Jason, going over to Michael and hugging him. "It makes you, like, a proper brother."

"Steady on, mate," said Michael. "Not in front of the genies!"

"I don't want to go back either, Jess." Jason turned to his sister. "I'm sorry."

Jess looked toward the shopwindow and out at the gray morning.

"Jess?" asked Milly.

"I did have my heart set on getting back to London. . . ." Jess spoke quietly and her eyes were far away. "I wanted to go back to our old lives so much. But after everything that's happened this last week . . . I guess it doesn't seem so important now."

"So, you don't want to go back either?" said Milly.

Jess took a deep breath. "No. London's not going anywhere. I'll go back one day. But in the meantime . . ." A grin broke out on her face. "I want to stay here!"

Milly gasped in relief and ran to hug her. Jason hugged her too. She pulled away and looked at Michael, suddenly uncertain.

"Oh, come here, you," said Michael. He grabbed Jess and swung her around. She squealed, sounding very much like Milly for a moment.

"Ow!" Skribble gasped loudly.

Everyone looked at him—and saw that the book was starting to shake.

"What's happening, Skribble?" Milly asked anxiously. "Is the book about to say something?"

"I don't think so!" Skribble gasped as silver and purple sparks began flying across the book's pages. He had to duck and dodge and dance to avoid them. "It's more than that! It's . . . *Oh!*" he gasped as the sparks zoomed together and formed lines of bright light in the air above the book. Then they began to swirl like a mini tornado. With a cry, Skribble was sucked out of the book and started floating helplessly up into the whirling haze of light.

"Skribble!" Milly shouted.

"Keep back!" gasped the bookworm.

The pages of the book below him turned and thrashed like an animal in pain. Faster and faster the blaze of light swirled until Skribble's body could barely be seen in its center.

"What's happening?" cried Jess.

Skribble's only answer was a heartrending scream.

Milly flung herself onto her knees as the light grew blindingly bright. "Stop it!" she begged Vega. "Whatever you're doing, stop it, please! He's been punished enough— save him before it's too late!"

Chapter Thirty-three

A smile flickered across Vega's face. "No, child. This is the way it must be."

Michael could just see the little worm's wide eyes through the swirling magic. "But what's happening to him?"

"What he has craved for almost two thousand years," Vega said softly. She moved closer to the blaze of light. It grew bigger and bigger, swirling up to the ceiling, and in the center of it, Milly and the others saw Skribble's shape begin to change. They caught the impression of a tall, thin man with a high forehead, the jutting twirls of an impressive moustache.

"What's going on?" Jess breathed.

"His magic is being restored," Sabik announced. "It would seem he has fulfilled the terms of his punishment."

"But how?" said Milly.

"He has helped all of you achieve your *true* heart's desires," Sabik said simply as the vortex of light grew wider and brighter still.

"But he didn't do any magic," said Michael, transfixed. "We didn't even make a wish."

"You did not need to," Vega told him. "The terms of Skribble's punishment stated that he would regain his powers if he helped a worthy subject *achieve* his heart's desire—and that he has done. . . ."

"I don't get it," said Michael.

"I do," said Jason slowly. "Our real hearts' desire wasn't to be genies or to go back to London. We just wanted to be happy, and we thought that those things would *make* us happy."

Milly looked up at Jess. "But now we're happier here in Moreways Meet, aren't we?"

Jess smiled. "So long as we have less frozen pizza, I guess so!"

"Keep this up and you two are gonna make me puke," Michael complained, but he was smiling as he said it.

"Whether great or small, true magic comes from within," said Vega. "Although his intentions were not noble, Skribble has helped you recognize what it is that you truly want."

"To make a go of being a proper family," Jess declared. "Wherever we happen to be living."

As she spoke, the light began to unravel from around Skribble. There was a silver flash and a puff of smoke and

Skribble was once again a bookworm.

He flopped onto the page, exhausted.

"I thought he was supposed to be a genie now," said Milly.

"Fear not," Vega told them. "Skribbaleum's powers have been fully restored—but he must remain in this body until he regains strength enough to revert to his true genie form."

Milly went cautiously over to the book. "Skribble?"

The bookworm lifted his head feebly, but did not speak.

"Take him from the paper," Sabik told Milly gently. "Both he and the book are awash now with many magics. These magics will intermingle and bind both together forever unless Skribbaleum is taken from the book at once. He must be placed somewhere safe while he recovers."

"Our lamp," said Jess quickly. "Put him in there, Milly."

"A fitting place," said Vega. She watched as Milly picked up the twitching bookworm, carried him over to their battered old genie lamp, and slipped him gently inside through the spout. As she did so, her genie costume seemed to shimmer about her—and suddenly she was back in her nightdress and rabbit slippers. She quickly saw that Michael, Jason, and Jess were back in their pajamas, too, and felt a pang of sadness mingled with relief that things could now get back to normal. *No,* Milly corrected herself, *not normal. Better than ever.*

"Hear me, Skribbaleum El Lazeez Ekir," Sabik rumbled. "Learn your lesson well and never again take your magic for granted. You have the power to achieve great things. Use that power well from this day on."

"And now . . ." Vega strode over and picked up the handbook. "It is time for us to leave you."

"And at last we can restore it to its rightful place in our library," said Vega. The book's pages fluttered gently, as if it was breathing out a sigh of relief.

"Bye, book," Milly said softly. "I'll miss you."

"You have not yet made your wish," Sabik reminded them. "What is it to be?"

"A pony—a real one I can ride," said Milly quickly.

"To go in a rocket," put in Jason.

"To be able to transport ourselves anywhere we want," said Michael.

"I want a nicer nose," Jess blurted out.

The others swung around.

"What do you want that for?" said Michael in astonishment.

"I—I just do."

He grinned. "You're mental."

Jess hesitated and then grinned back. "Look who's talking!"

Sabik frowned impatiently. "Enough of this dalliance. Our time is short. If you cannot decide, you must leave it to us to judge what it is that you need."

"Hey, wait a minute—" Michael began.

But Vega had already turned to a bookshelf in the art section behind them. *"As we take so shall we give!"*

A ball of blazing light shot out from her finger. It hit the shelf and exploded in a cloud of sparks. All the children gasped and jumped back as a brown leather book appeared on the shelf. Its cover was smoking slightly.

Then Sabik turned and aimed a bolt of white light at the back of the shop. It burst into silver sparks as it shot past the map section.

"Please don't wreck the place," Jason begged. "It's not even open yet."

Vega smiled, her eyes catlike and glittering. Then she took hold of her lamp, and Sabik took hold of his.

"Perhaps one day we shall meet again," said Sabik to the children. "Farewell." With a mysterious smile he clapped his hands and both he and Vega vanished in a puff of gold smoke.

Jess stared. "This is just too, too weird."

"What else is new?" said Michael. "I can't believe all

they've left us is some rubbishy, boring book." He picked it up. "It's all in Latin or ancient Greek or something equally dumb."

"It's got pictures in it," said Milly, looking at painted scenes of animals and the stars and funny-looking people bathing in streams. "They're a bit strange, though. It's not much of a swap for *The Genie Handbook*!"

Jason frowned. "Could it be magic?"

"Nah," said Michael. "Can't even read the title. Typical genie trick—it's just an old art book." He shoved the book on a shelf and looked down at his robe, thoughtfully. "But you know, maybe that's a good thing! It's been fun having the handbook, but, well . . ."

"It'll be nice for things to just be quiet for a while," Jess put in.

Michael smiled. "Until Skribble recovers, at least!"

"While we're waiting, I can go riding with Emily," said Milly.

Jess nodded. "And I can get to know Colette, Jodie, and Natasha better. Go shopping and have sleepovers!"

"Maybe I can get Sarah Sellick's phone number," said Michael thoughtfully. Jess elbowed him. "Hey!" He grinned. "Okay, maybe I can go around to Ben's and play Maximum Carnage—the nonmagic version! Jess can get Colette to nick all the best new games off Ollie. . . ." He winked at Jason. "You can come too if you want, Jase."

Jason beamed. "I can?"

Just then there was the sound of a key turning in the lock of the shop door.

"It's Ann and Dad!" Milly gasped. "They must be here to get ready for the opening!"

"What are we going to say—" Jess began, but it was too late for discussion. Ann and Mark were already coming into the shop, their arms laden with bags and boxes. They stopped dead when they saw the children.

"Whatever are you lot doing here at seven thirty in the morning?" Ann exclaimed. "And in your pajamas?"

"We thought you were all still in bed," said Mark. "We wanted to make a start on the preparations, and sneaked out of the house so we wouldn't wake you!"

"Er, we sneaked out, too, so we wouldn't wake *you*!" said Jess quickly. "We were so excited about the opening, we couldn't sleep. . . ."

"And so we thought we'd come down and make sure everything was clean and tidy," Milly added. "You know, dust the books . . ."

"Help get everything ready," Jason chimed in.

Michael cleared his throat. "And we didn't want to get our clothes dirty, so we, um, didn't bother getting dressed."

Ann's face was darkening. "But you're not even wear-ing shoes!"

"We, uh . . ." Jason racked his brain for a convincing explanation. "That is to say, we—"

"Hey! Wow!" Mark had walked down to the map sec-tion at the back to dump his bags, and now was staring around in delighted amazement. "You kids might be crazy, but you've done a great job!"

"We have?" Michael said, shooting a *what's-going-on* look at the others.

They followed Mark and gasped. The back of the shop was now decorated with gold and purple banners and streamers and a big sign saying, GRAND OPENING!

"Oh, my goodness!" said Ann, her frown fading as she joined them. "It's amazing. Thank you!" She hugged them all. "Where did you get the stuff from? How did you do it?"

Jess gave a helpless shrug of her shoulders.

"I suppose we're just . . . magic!" said Milly.

Ann's eyes were shining. "Well, it's wonderful."

Mark nodded. "Thanks so much, kids!"

Milly went over and hugged him. "So we're all ready to open then, Dad?"

"All ready?" Mark shook his head. "Nowhere near! There are the carpets to vacuum, the plates and glasses to collect, the nibbles to go into bowls, cash to go into the tills. . . ."

Jess grinned. "And clothes to go onto us!"

"Then what are we waiting for?" Michael slapped his dad on the back. "Give us a lift home so we can change, yeah? Then let's get on with making this the best bookshop opening ever!"

Chapter Thirty-four

"Ginny, it's great to see you! Come in!"

"More wine, David?"

"Mum! Come over here. Colette's mum wants to meet you."

"Emily! Hi! Come and look at the horse books with me!"

"Yo, Ben!"

The Worthingtons' voices rose above the buzz of chatter in the bookshop. The grand opening had started at two o'clock. It was now an hour later and the shop was full of people. They were chatting and drinking wine and orange juice, eating crisps and browsing the bookshelves.

"I can't believe there are so many people here," Ann said as she rang up a purchase at the till and smiled at the customer. "Thanks very much."

"Mum!" Jess said for about the third time. "Colette's mum really wants to say hi!"

"Okay, okay, I'm coming!" Ann said. "Mark, can you

take over on the till?"

Leaving Michael to pour out drinks, Mark took his wife's place at the cash desk. "This is turning out better than I ever expected," he said to Jason, who was straightening the little comedy books by the till point.

"Look, there's Sarah Sellick." Jason pointed as the journalist came into the shop.

"Hi, guys," she said, walking over. "Just thought I'd call in and see how it's going." She brandished a camera. "Do you mind if I take a few photos for the paper? I'll run a short piece on the opening."

"Great!" Mark said, looking delighted. "Snap away." He looked around at the crowd of people and sighed happily. "This is a dream come true for me, Jason, mate. I'm so glad we moved here."

"So are we," said Jason.

"Good." Mark turned to greet another customer, a contented smile sitting easily on his face.

Jason saw Milly over by the refreshments table and joined her. "It's going really well, isn't it?"

She nodded. "I hope Skribble's okay with all the noise." They looked over to the shelf they had left the lamp on in the nonfiction section. "Maybe we should check?"

They both went over. Ginny was looking at a book there.

"Oh, no, no, no!" a familiar voice was muttering. "You'd do much better choosing a book about something sensible."

Ginny frowned slightly and then rubbed her head as if it was hurting. She put down a book about soap operas and picked up the one next to it: *Magic in the Entertainment Industry.*

"Much better," the voice said approvingly.

Looking bemused and slightly dazed, Ginny headed off for the till.

"Skribble!" Milly hissed, going over to the lamp. "You mustn't talk to the customers!"

Jason caught sight of the worm's head at the top of the lamp's spout. "Milly's right. People will find out about you!"

"Foolish boy!" Skribble snapped. "You know a person must believe in magic before he or she can hear my voice properly. Have you learned nothing over the course of your training?" He gave a loud, indignant sniff. "Really!"

Milly giggled. It sounded like Skribble was back to his old self! "You're feeling better, then?"

"I am very much recovered, thank you, Milly." Skribble sighed. "Soon, I will leave you."

"Not yet!" Milly blurted out. "You can't!" Several people turned to look at her in surprise. She fixed a grin on her face. "I mean, you *can't* get more orange juice out yet, Jason!"

The people turned away again, and Milly and Jason looked back at Skribble.

"I'm afraid I *must* go, my dear Milly." Skribble's voice was softer now. "My work here is done, and my punishment at an end. It is time to move on."

"Please, Skribble," Milly begged. "Stay just a little while longer, until everyone goes and we can say good-bye properly."

"Very well." The line of the bookworm's mouth slid into a smile. "I will delay my parting for a short while." He crawled back into the lamp, a happy look in his eyes.

"I don't want him to go," sighed Milly.

"Me neither," Jason said. "But I guess he has to."

Milly nodded slowly. And then she noticed a man, quite old, dressed in a corduroy jacket with a black polo neck underneath. He had graying hair and a wise, lined face, and was browsing the shelves in the secondhand art section. Milly noticed his eyes settle on the book that Sabik and Vega had left before parting. He picked it off the shelf, and as he read the title he blinked.

He turned the volume over in his hands, opened up the cover.

"I forgot about that thing," Jason whispered. "Do you

think he's going to buy it?"

Before Milly could speak, the man gave a quick, sharp gasp. He looked through the pages of the book and started shaking his head. "Definitely post-medieval parchment, quires of eight leaves . . . No! Surely, it can't be . . ."

"What's wrong with it?" Milly whispered. "Why's he looking like that? Is it magic? A genie trick?"

Jason gulped. "We should never have left it on the shelves! We should have hidden it. Oh, Milly—"

Mark was passing by and overheard the man's mutterings. "Hello," he said. "I'm Mark Worthington. I co-own this shop. Is there a problem?"

"Not a problem." The man took the book in both hands and looked wonderingly at the cover. "Just a miracle. This book—*The Book of Hours, for Use in Rouen-de-Lys.* Where did you find it?"

"That's from . . ." Mark looked at the cover of the book and frowned. "Actually, I . . . I don't quite recognize it. How terrible. I picked some boxes of books up from a house clearance last weekend; I imagine it was one of those. What is it?"

"What *is* it?" The other man stared at him. "It's an illuminated manuscript—early eighteenth century, I should say. It contains religious texts and calendars and prayers and . . . it's in such amazing condition! I've never seen anything like it!"

Milly didn't have a clue what he was going on about. But her dad looked totally shocked.

"Then . . ." Mark swallowed. "Surely that must be quite rare."

"It's *exceedingly* rare, my friend!" The man grinned, looking equally astonished. He pulled a card out of his top pocket. "I happen to be an expert on books of this era. My name is John Underwood."

"A professor of history," Mark said, reading the card. "Lucky you came along when you did!"

Jason whispered to Milly: "Luck had nothing to do with it—but I bet Sabik and Vega did!"

The man nodded. "I must tell you, Mr. Worthington, this book is of immense value. At auction you might expect it to fetch a six-figure sum."

"For one book?" Mark went pale. "Goodness, that's very honest of you. . . . You could have bought it for next to nothing and I wouldn't have known any better!"

The professor just smiled. "If you wish to sell it, Mr. Worthington, I can put you in touch with some people and organizations who would give you a fair price. . . ."

"Well . . . I . . . yes! Yes, please!" Mark babbled. "Ann! Ann!"

Ann hurried over. "What's up?"

As Mark explained, Jess and Michael joined Jason and Milly. "What *is* up?" Jess wondered.

Milly was bouncing up and down with excitement. "That book the genies left is worth loads of money!"

The news of the valuable book spread around the shop like wildfire. Everyone crowded around.

Sarah squeezed her way to the front, camera in hand, and marched up to Professor Underwood. "What a great story!" she exclaimed. "I'm Sarah Sellick from the *Moreways Gazette*. So, this really is a rare book? You think collectors might buy it?"

"Collectors will most *definitely* want to buy it!" Professor Underwood announced.

Ann gave Mark a delighted look. "Think of the debts we can pay off!"

"I could get in the *national* press with this," said Sarah, whisking out her tape recorder. "Could you give me a quick interview, Professor?"

"Certainly," the professor replied. "It would seem that this is a very special day!"

Mark turned to Ann. "You can say that again."

"It's amazing!" Ann said. "And it's not just the money. Think of all the publicity we'll get!"

"And *then* think of the money!" Michael grinned. "Can I have a Megaplay Ultra then, Dad?"

"And a really big TV for us to play it on," said Jason.

Mark laughed. "If you're lucky!"

"And I'd love to go shopping in London with Colette one day," said Jess.

Ann grinned. "I don't see why not."

"Can I have a pony?" begged Milly.

"No!" Ann said firmly. "But you *can* have riding lessons."

"I can go with Emily, and maybe ride Pepper!" Milly's eyes grew as wide as saucers. "Oh, wow," she breathed. "Oh . . . oh . . . *wow*!"

Just then Sarah came over. "Can I have a picture of you all together?" She started arranging them in a group. "There we are."

Milly's eyes fell on the lamp that Skribble was in. It was still on the shelf. "Wait!" she cried, dashing across the room. "Can this be in the picture?"

"Hey, I had a lamp that looked a bit like that." Ann looked around in surprise. "But I can't seem to find it. . . ."

"Never mind, eh?" said Michael quickly.

"We bought this one at the junk shop." Milly opened her eyes wide and gave Ann her sweetest smile. "I thought it looked like it might have a genie inside. . . ."

Ann smiled back. "You have such a vivid imagination,

Milly. Well, I don't see why it can't be in the picture, too."
She turned to put her arm around Mark's waist. He rested
his cheek happily against her hair.

"Okay. All ready?" said Sarah. "Say cheese—" She
broke off as she looked at the lamp. "No, I know. Say
'genie' instead!"

Michael, Jess, Jason, and Milly exchanged grins.

"Your wish is our command," said Michael.

"After three, then," Sarah said. "One . . . two . . .
three!"

"Genie!" everyone yelled. And just as the camera
flashed, Milly was sure she saw a worm's head—unseen
by grown-up eyes—poke out from the spout of the lamp,
its tiny line of a mouth stretched into a proud smile.

Chapter Thirty-five

"A bath and a night watching telly for me," Ann said as they locked up the shop after their final customers. "I'm shattered."

"Me too!" Mark yawned. "How about you kids?"

Milly touched the lamp in her bag.

"We've got some stuff to do," said Jess, glancing at the others.

Michael nodded. "A game to finish playing."

When they got back to the house, the four of them went into the den. Milly placed the lamp in the middle of the floor. She could hardly believe it was time to say good-bye to Skribble.

"So this is it?" Jess said softly, looking at the lamp.

"How do we get him out?" wondered Michael.

"Get him out? Get him out! Of all the nerve!" Skribble exclaimed from inside the lamp. "Would you squeeze a butterfly from its cocoon before it is properly prepared? I am Skribbaleum El Lazeez Ekir! I will emerge when I am ready!" There was a moment's pause and then the bookworm's little head popped out from the spout. "Well, here I am," he announced, staring around at them all.

For a few seconds no one seemed to know what to say.

"Good-bye," said Skribble abruptly.

Jess swallowed. "Good-bye."

"Yeah, see you, Worm," said Michael awkwardly.

Jason nodded. "Bye, Skribble."

Milly looked at the little bookworm's gruff face and a sob suddenly burst from her. "Oh, Skribble," she said, dropping to her knees. "I don't want you to go. I don't want to say good-bye."

Skribble's expression softened. "I do not wish it either. But I *must* leave. My magic is restored and I can now transform into my true genie form."

"But can't you do that and still stay with us?" Milly pleaded. "You could live in the lamp and grant us wishes and—"

"No," Skribble broke in gently. "It is not possible, dear Milly."

"Why not?"

"If I were to give you wish after wish, you would have nothing to strive for. It would not lead to happiness for either you or those around you. You would grow lazy and arrogant. . . ." He sighed. "Just as I did."

"All right, forget the wishes," said Milly. "I don't care about them. But please stay!"

"I cannot," Skribble told her. "My work in the human world is not yet done. If I am to make amends for my laziness in the past, I must impress the Genie High Council with my verve and my wit and my extraordinary magical talents." He cleared his throat and smiled. "Therefore, I intend to stay awhile in the human world. And with your permission, I would like to use this lamp as my vessel."

"Of course," Jess said, and the others all nodded.

Tears prickled Milly's eyes. "But . . . will we ever see you again?"

Skribble puffed out his cheeks. "Time will tell . . . yes, time will tell." He nodded sagely to himself. "Our paths have crossed, and all our lives are the better for it. But now we must take different roads. That is the way it is, and the way it should be. It is written in the . . ."

"Small print?" said Michael with a sigh.

Skribble shook his head. "No. In the stars."

The lump in Milly's throat was too big to swallow back any longer. As she reached out and gently touched the side of Skribble's face, tears rolled down her cheeks. "I'll miss you," she whispered. "I'll really, really miss you."

"And I will miss you, too," he told her as Jess sniffed and Jason chewed his lower lip. "All of you. Wise Jason . . .

brave Jess . . . clever, kindhearted Milly, and . . ." He paused and fixed Michael with a look. "Yes, even you, the older boy. Impertinent, incorrigible—and ingenious Michael."

Michael took a deep breath and rubbed crossly at his eye. "Yeah, well. As worms go, you're the coolest I've ever met, okay?"

Skribble inclined his head. "I believe that is a compliment in the ridiculous modern language you use. Thank you." Then the old, imperious tone crept back into his voice. "Now, before I leave, I must ask one favor of you. When I change myself into my genie form, will one of you kindly summon me and make a wish—wish that the lamp would return to the shop in which you found it? Perhaps then, one day, someone worthy"—a small smile played across his face—"or someone *unworthy*, will find it. And then my work can begin."

"Okay," said Michael. "But as last wishes go, it's a bit boring!"

"Do this for me, children," said Skribble, "and I will grant you an extra wish of your own as a parting gift."

Milly wiped her eyes and grinned. "Thank you, lovely Skribble!"

The bookworm crawled out of the spout and dropped to the carpet in a tight ball. "And now there is but one thing left to do." Uncurling, he smiled at each of them in turn. "One set of adventures is over. Another is beginning. And as the saying goes . . . *Genie me!*"

There was a bright gold flash. The next instant, Skribble had gone. Only the lamp still stood there.

They all stared at it. It looked so old and ordinary.

"He's inside," whispered Jason. "As a *genie*."

"I wonder what he'll look like?" said Milly.

Michael shrugged. "Let's rub the lamp and find out."

"Milly should do it," suggested Jess.

"Oh, yes, can I?" Milly said excitedly.

Jason and Michael nodded.

"But you have to wish for something that we *all* want," Michael told her. "No wishing for a pony or something dumb like that."

Milly thought for a moment and then smiled. "Okay." She picked up the lamp and, holding it on her knee, rubbed her fingers across its engraved sides.

A glare of white light and a cloud of sparkling smoke burst out of its spout. As the light faded and the smoke cleared, a figure appeared in the air before her, floating on a cloud.

Everyone stared, speechless in amazement.

Skribble had come back to them in the guise of . . . a bookworm!

He had not changed at all—except that now he was

wearing a tiny turquoise turban and a blue silk cape, with a thin black moustache drooping down from his top lip.

"Do not be afraid," said Skribble, bobbing about on his cloud. "It is only me."

"Duh! Of course it's you!" Michael spluttered.

"You look exactly the same!" exclaimed Jess.

"Don't be ridiculous!" Skribble scowled. "My disguise is impenetrable!"

"But, Skribble," said Jason meekly, "why haven't you come back in your true form?"

"My true form was that of a falsehearted man," Skribble replied. "And so, until my work is done, a humble book-worm I shall remain." He lowered his voice and spoke confidentially. "I rather think the Genie High Council will like that little touch!"

Michael grinned. "You old faker."

"Maybe he is," said Milly fondly. "But he's brilliant."

"Now," Skribble boomed. "What is your wish, child?"

"I wish that the lamp was back on display in Junk and Disorderly with you safely inside it," said Milly. "And . . . and I wish . . ." Her voice wavered.

Jess squeezed Milly's fingers and nodded encouragement.

"I wish that none of us shall ever forget a single moment

of this whole adventure," Milly whispered. "That the memories stay bright and clear forever and ever, even when we're old and gray."

Skribble's beady black eyes looked deep into her own. "You will never forget," he murmured with a smile. "And neither shall I." Then he raised his voice and his eyes to the heavens. "*As you wish it, so shall it be!*"

A cloud of silver and gold sparkles exploded from the lamp's spout like fireworks. They shot into the air and then surrounded Skribble like a sparkling, glittering tornado. For a brief second, the bookworm's shape was still visible, floating on his cloud. He winked at the children and then he—and the sparkles—scattered into a million points of light, leaving just a faint trail of smoke in their wake.

"He's gone," Jason said, staring at the space where the bookworm had been.

"Happy travels, Worm." Michael swallowed hard. "And the best of luck to whoever rubs that lamp!"

"I wish it could be me." Milly turned to Jess and flung her arms around her.

Jess hugged her back. "Hey," she whispered. "It's okay."

Milly sniffed and nodded. "We'll see him again. I *know* we will."

"In the meantime, that was a pretty cool exit." Jason smiled.

"Cool and clever," agreed Jess.

"Clever?" Michael watched the last of the smoke drift away to nothing and grinned at the others. "That's not clever. That's *genie-us*!"